Don Quixote

by Miguel de Cervantes (1547-1616)

Published in 1605 in Spanish

Translated to English by John Ormsby (1829-1895) in 1885

Idle reader: thou mayest believe me without any oath that I would this book, as it is the child of my brain, were the fairest, gayest, and cleverest that could be imagined. But I could not counteract Nature's law that everything shall beget its like; and what, then, could this sterile, illtilled wit of mine beget but the story of a dry, shrivelled, whimsical offspring, full of thoughts of all sorts and such as never came into any other imagination—just what might be begotten in a prison, where every misery is lodged and every doleful sound makes its dwelling? Tranquillity, a cheerful retreat, pleasant fields, bright skies, murmuring brooks, peace of mind, these are the things that go far to make even the most barren muses fertile, and bring into the world births that fill it with wonder and delight. Sometimes when a father has an ugly, loutish son, the love he bears him so blindfolds his eyes that he does not see his defects, or, rather, takes them for gifts and charms of mind and body, and talks of them to his friends as wit and grace. I, however—for though I pass for the father, I am but the stepfather to "Don Quixote"—have no desire to go with the current of custom, or to implore thee, dearest reader, almost with tears in my eyes, as others do, to pardon or excuse the defects thou wilt perceive in this child of mine. Thou art neither its kinsman nor its friend, thy soul is thine own and thy will as free as any man's, whate'er he be, thou art in thine own house and master of it as much as the king of his taxes and thou knowest the common saying, "Under my cloak I kill the king;" all which exempts and frees thee from every consideration and obligation, and thou canst say what thou wilt of the story without fear of being abused for any ill or rewarded for any good thou mayest say of it.

My wish would be simply to present it to thee plain and unadorned, without any embellishment of preface or uncountable muster of customary sonnets, epigrams, and eulogies, such as are commonly put at the beginning of books. For I can tell thee, though composing it cost me some labour, I found none greater than the making of this Preface thou art now reading. Many times did I take up my pen to write it, and many did I lay it down again, not knowing what to write. One of these times, as I was pondering with the paper before me, a pen in my ear, my elbow on the desk, and my cheek in my hand, thinking of what I should say, there came in unexpectedly a certain lively, clever friend of mine, who, seeing me so deep in thought, asked the reason; to which I, making no mystery of it, answered that I was thinking of the Preface I had to make for the story of "Don Quixote," which so troubled me that I had a mind not to make any at all, nor even publish the achievements of so noble a knight.

"For, how could you expect me not to feel uneasy about what that ancient lawgiver they call the Public will say when it sees me, after slumbering so many years in the silence of oblivion, coming out now with all my years upon my back, and with a book as dry as a rush, devoid of invention, meagre in style, poor in thoughts, wholly wanting in learning and wisdom, without quotations in the margin or annotations at the end, after the fashion of other books I see, which, though all fables and profanity, are so full of maxims from Aristotle, and Plato, and the whole herd of philosophers, that they fill the readers with amazement and convince them that the authors are men of learning, erudition, and eloquence. And then, when they quote the Holy Scriptures!—anyone would say they are St. Thomases or other doctors of the Church, observing as they do a decorum so ingenious that in one sentence they describe a distracted lover and in the next deliver a devout little sermon that it is a pleasure and a treat to hear and read. Of all this there will be nothing in my book, for I have nothing to quote in the margin or to note at the end, and still less do I know what authors I follow in it, to place them at the beginning, as all do, under the letters A, B, C, beginning with Aristotle and ending with Xenophon, or Zoilus, or Zeuxis, though one was a slanderer and the other a painter. Also my book must do without sonnets at the beginning, at least sonnets whose authors are dukes, marquises, counts, bishops, ladies, or famous poets. Though if I were to ask two or three obliging friends, I know they would give me them, and such as the productions of those that have the highest reputation in our Spain could not equal.

"In short, my friend," I continued, "I am determined that Senor Don Quixote shall remain buried in the archives of his own La Mancha until Heaven provide some one to garnish him with all those things he stands in need of; because I find myself, through my shallowness and want of learning, unequal to supplying them, and because I am by nature shy and careless about hunting for authors to say what I myself can say without them. Hence the cogitation and abstraction you found me in, and reason enough, what you have heard from me."

Hearing this, my friend, giving himself a slap on the forehead and breaking into a hearty laugh, exclaimed, "Before God, Brother, now am I disabused of an error in which I have been living all this long time I have known you, all through which I have taken you to be shrewd and sensible in all you do; but now I see you are as far from that as the heaven is from the earth. It is possible that things of so little moment and so easy to set right can occupy and perplex a ripe wit like yours, fit to break through and crush far greater obstacles? By my faith, this comes, not of any want of ability, but of too much indolence and too little knowledge of life. Do you want to know if I am telling the truth? Well, then, attend to me, and you will see how, in the opening and shutting of an eye, I sweep away all your difficulties, and supply all those deficiencies which you say check and discourage you from bringing before the world the story of your famous Don Quixote, the light and mirror of all knight-errantry."

"Say on," said I, listening to his talk; "how do you propose to make up for my diffidence, and reduce to order this chaos of perplexity I am in?"

To which he made answer, "Your first difficulty about the sonnets, epigrams, or complimentary verses which you want for the beginning, and which ought to be by persons of importance and rank, can be removed if you yourself take a little trouble to make them; you can afterwards baptise them, and put any name you like to them, fathering them on Prester John of the Indies or the Emperor of Trebizond, who, to my knowledge, were said to have been famous poets: and even if they were not, and any pedants or bachelors should attack you and question the fact, never care two maravedis for that, for even if they prove a lie against you they cannot cut off the hand you wrote it with.

"As to references in the margin to the books and authors from whom you take the aphorisms and sayings you put into your story, it is only contriving to fit in nicely any sentences or scraps of Latin you may happen to have by heart, or at any rate that will not give you much trouble to look up; so as, when you speak of freedom and captivity, to insert

Non bene pro toto libertas venditur auro;

and then refer in the margin to Horace, or whoever said it; or, if you allude to the power of death, to come in with—

Pallida mors Aequo pulsat pede pauperum tabernas, Regumque turres.

"If it be friendship and the love God bids us bear to our enemy, go at once to the Holy Scriptures, which you can do with a very small amount of research, and quote no less than the words of God himself: Ego autem dico vobis: diligite inimicos vestros. If you speak of evil thoughts, turn to the Gospel: De corde exeunt cogitationes malae. If of the fickleness of friends, there is Cato, who will give you his distich:

Donec eris felix multos numerabis amicos, Tempora si fuerint nubila, solus eris.

"With these and such like bits of Latin they will take you for a grammarian at all events, and that now-a-days is no small honour and profit.

"With regard to adding annotations at the end of the book, you may safely do it in this way. If you mention any giant in your book contrive that it shall be the giant Goliath, and with this alone, which will cost you almost nothing, you have a grand note, for you can put—The giant Golias or Goliath was a Philistine whom the shepherd David slew by a mighty stone-cast in the Terebinth valley, as is related in the Book of Kings—in the chapter where you find it written.

"Next, to prove yourself a man of erudition in polite literature and cosmography, manage that the river Tagus shall be named in your story, and there you are at once with another famous annotation, setting forth—The river Tagus was so called after a King of Spain: it has its source in such and such a place and falls into the ocean, kissing the walls of the famous city of Lisbon, and it is a common belief that it has golden sands, etc. If you should have anything to do with robbers, I will give you the story of Cacus, for I have it by heart; if with loose women, there is the Bishop of Mondonedo, who will give you the loan of

Lamia, Laida, and Flora, any reference to whom will bring you great credit; if with hard-hearted ones, Ovid will furnish you with Medea; if with witches or enchantresses, Homer has Calypso, and Virgil Circe; if with valiant captains, Julius Caesar himself will lend you himself in his own 'Commentaries,' and Plutarch will give you a thousand Alexanders. If you should deal with love, with two ounces you may know of Tuscan you can go to Leon the Hebrew, who will supply you to your heart's content; or if you should not care to go to foreign countries you have at home Fonseca's 'Of the Love of God,' in which is condensed all that you or the most imaginative mind can want on the subject. In short, all you have to do is to manage to quote these names, or refer to these stories I have mentioned, and leave it to me to insert the annotations and quotations, and I swear by all that's good to fill your margins and use up four sheets at the end of the book.

"Now let us come to those references to authors which other books have, and you want for yours. The remedy for this is very simple: You have only to look out for some book that quotes them all, from A to Z as you say yourself, and then insert the very same alphabet in your book, and though the imposition may be plain to see, because you have so little need to borrow from them, that is no matter; there will probably be some simple enough to believe that you have made use of them all in this plain, artless story of yours. At any rate, if it answers no other purpose, this long catalogue of authors will serve to give a surprising look of authority to your book. Besides, no one will trouble himself to verify whether you have followed them or whether you have not, being no way concerned in it; especially as, if I mistake not, this book of yours has no need of any one of those things you say it wants, for it is, from beginning to end, an attack upon the books of chivalry, of which Aristotle never dreamt, nor St. Basil said a word, nor Cicero had any knowledge; nor do the niceties of truth nor the observations of astrology come within the range of its fanciful vagaries; nor have geometrical measurements or refutations of the arguments used in rhetoric anything to do with it; nor does it mean to preach to anybody, mixing up things human and divine, a sort of motley in which no Christian understanding should dress itself. It has only to avail itself of truth to nature in its composition, and the more perfect the imitation the better the work will be. And as this piece of yours aims at nothing more than to destroy the authority and influence which books of chivalry have in the world and with the public, there is no need for you to go a-begging for aphorisms from philosophers, precepts from Holy Scripture, fables from poets, speeches from orators, or miracles from saints; but merely to take care that your style and diction run musically, pleasantly, and plainly, with clear, proper, and well-placed words, setting forth your purpose to the best of your power, and putting your ideas intelligibly, without confusion or obscurity. Strive, too, that in reading your story the melancholy may be moved to laughter, and the merry made merrier still; that the simple shall not be wearied, that the judicious shall admire the invention, that the grave shall not despise it, nor the wise fail to praise it. Finally, keep your aim fixed on the destruction of that ill-founded edifice of the books of chivalry, hated by some and praised by many more; for if you succeed in this you will have achieved no small success."

In profound silence I listened to what my friend said, and his observations made such an impression on me that, without attempting to question them, I admitted their soundness, and out of them I determined to make this Preface; wherein, gentle reader, thou wilt perceive my friend's good sense, my good fortune in finding such an adviser in such a time of need, and what thou hast gained in receiving, without addition or alteration, the story of the famous Don Quixote of La Mancha, who is held by all the inhabitants of the district of the Campo de Montiel to have been the chastest lover and the bravest knight that has for many years been seen in that neighbourhood. I have no desire to magnify the service I render thee in making thee acquainted with so renowned and honoured a knight, but I do desire thy thanks for the acquaintance thou wilt make with the famous Sancho Panza, his squire, in whom, to my thinking, I have given thee condensed all the squirely drolleries that are scattered through the swarm of the vain books of chivalry. And so—may God give thee health, and not forget me. Vale.

DEDICATION OF VOLUME I

TO THE DUKE OF BEJAR, MARQUIS OF GIBRALEON, COUNT OF BENALCAZAR AND BANARES, VICECOUNT OF THE PUEBLA DE ALCOCER, MASTER OF THE TOWNS OF CAPILLA, CURIEL AND BURGUILLOS

In belief of the good reception and honours that Your Excellency bestows on all sort of books, as prince so inclined to favor good arts, chiefly those who by their nobleness do not submit to the service and bribery of the vulgar, I have determined bringing to light The Ingenious Gentleman Don Quixote of la Mancha, in shelter of Your Excellency's glamorous name, to whom, with the obeisance I owe to such grandeur, I pray to receive it agreeably under his protection, so that in this shadow, though deprived of that precious ornament of elegance and erudition that clothe the works composed in the houses of those who know, it dares appear with assurance in the judgment of some who, trespassing the bounds of their own ignorance, use to condemn with more rigour and less justice the writings of others. It is my earnest hope that Your Excellency's good counsel in regard to my honourable purpose, will not disdain the littleness of so humble a service.

Miguel de Cervantes

VOLUME I.

CHAPTER I.

WHICH TREATS OF THE CHARACTER AND PURSUITS OF THE FAMOUS GENTLEMAN DON QUIXOTE OF LA MANCHA

In a village of La Mancha, the name of which I have no desire to call to mind, there lived not long since one of those gentlemen that keep a lance in the lance-rack, an old buckler, a lean hack, and a greyhound for coursing. An olla of rather more beef than mutton, a salad on most nights, scraps on Saturdays, lentils on Fridays, and a pigeon or so extra on Sundays, made away with three-quarters of his income. The rest of it went in a doublet of fine cloth and velvet breeches and shoes to match for holidays, while on week-days he made a brave figure in his best homespun. He had in his house a housekeeper past forty, a niece under twenty, and a lad for the field and market-place, who used to saddle the hack as well as handle the bill-hook. The age of this gentleman of ours was bordering on fifty; he was of a hardy habit, spare, gaunt-featured, a very early riser and a great sportsman. They will have it his surname was Quixada or Quesada (for here there is some difference of opinion among the authors who write on the subject), although from reasonable conjectures it seems plain that he was called Quexana. This, however, is of but little importance to our tale; it will be enough not to stray a hair's breadth from the truth in the telling of it.

You must know, then, that the above-named gentleman whenever he was at leisure (which was mostly all the year round) gave himself up to reading books of chivalry with such ardour and avidity that he almost entirely neglected the pursuit of his field-sports, and even the management of his property; and to such a pitch did his eagerness and infatuation go that he sold many an acre of tillageland to buy books of chivalry to read, and brought home as many of them as he could get. But of all there were none he liked so well as those of the famous Feliciano de Silva's composition, for their lucidity of style and complicated conceits were as pearls in his sight, particularly when in his reading he came upon courtships and cartels, where he often found passages like "the reason of the unreason with which my reason is afflicted so weakens my reason that with reason I murmur at your beauty;" or again, "the high heavens, that of your divinity divinely fortify you with the stars, render you deserving of the desert your greatness deserves." Over conceits of this sort the poor gentleman lost his wits, and used to lie awake striving to understand them and worm the meaning out of them; what Aristotle himself could not have made out or extracted had he come to life again for that special purpose. He was not at all easy about the wounds which Don Belianis gave and took, because it seemed to him that, great as were the surgeons who had cured him, he must have had his face and body covered all over with seams and scars. He commended, however, the author's way of ending his book with the promise of that interminable adventure, and many a time was he tempted to take up his pen and finish it properly as is there proposed, which no doubt he would have done, and made a successful piece of work of it too, had not greater and more absorbing thoughts prevented him.

Many an argument did he have with the curate of his village (a learned man, and a graduate of Siguenza) as to which had been the better knight, Palmerin of England or Amadis of Gaul. Master Nicholas, the village barber, however, used to say that neither of them came up to the Knight of Phoebus, and that if there was any that could compare with him it was Don Galaor, the brother of Amadis of Gaul, because he had a spirit that was equal to every occasion, and was no finikin knight, nor lachrymose like his brother, while in the matter of valour he was not a whit behind him. In short, he became so absorbed in his books that he spent his nights from sunset to sunrise, and his days from dawn to dark, poring over them; and what with little sleep and much reading his brains got so dry that he lost his wits. His fancy grew full of what he used to read about in his books, enchantments, quarrels, battles, challenges, wounds, wooings, loves, agonies, and all sorts of impossible nonsense; and it so possessed his mind that the whole fabric of invention and fancy he read of was true, that to him no history in the world had more reality in it. He used to say the Cid Ruy Diaz was a very good knight, but that he was not to be compared with the Knight of the Burning Sword who with one back-stroke cut in half two fierce and monstrous giants. He thought more of Bernardo del Carpio because at Roncesvalles he slew Roland in spite of enchantments, availing himself of the artifice of Hercules when he strangled Antaeus the son of Terra in his arms. He approved highly of the giant Morgante, because, although of the giant breed which is always arrogant and ill-conditioned, he alone was affable and well-bred. But above all he admired Reinaldos of Montalban, especially when he saw him sallying forth from his castle and robbing everyone he met, and when beyond the seas he stole that image of Mahomet which, as his history says, was entirely of gold. To have a bout of kicking at that traitor of a Ganelon he would have given his housekeeper, and his niece into the bargain.

In short, his wits being quite gone, he hit upon the strangest notion that ever madman in this world hit upon, and that was that he fancied it was right and requisite, as well for the support of his own honour as for the service of his country, that he should make a knight-errant of himself, roaming the world over in full armour and on horseback in quest of adventures, and putting in practice himself all that he had read of as being the usual practices of knights-errant; righting every kind of wrong, and exposing himself to peril and danger from which, in the issue, he was to reap eternal renown and fame. Already the poor man saw himself crowned by the might of his arm Emperor of Trebizond at least; and so, led away by the intense enjoyment he found in these pleasant fancies, he set himself forthwith to put his scheme into execution.

The first thing he did was to clean up some armour that had belonged to his great-grandfather, and had been for ages lying forgotten in a corner eaten with rust and covered with mildew. He scoured and polished it as best he could, but he perceived one great defect in it, that it had no closed helmet, nothing but a simple morion. This deficiency, however, his ingenuity supplied, for he contrived a kind of half-helmet of pasteboard which, fitted on to the morion, looked like a whole one. It is true that, in order to see if it was strong and fit to stand a cut, he drew his sword and gave it a couple of slashes, the first of which undid in an instant what had taken him a week to do. The ease with which he had knocked it to pieces disconcerted him somewhat, and to guard against that danger he set to work again, fixing bars of iron on the inside until he was satisfied with its strength; and then, not caring to try any more experiments with it, he passed it and adopted it as a helmet of the most perfect construction.

He next proceeded to inspect his hack, which, with more quartos than a real and more blemishes than the steed of Gonela, that "tantum pellis et ossa fuit," surpassed in his eyes the Bucephalus of Alexander or the Babieca of the Cid. Four days were spent in thinking what name to give him, because (as he said to himself) it was not right that a horse belonging to a knight so famous, and one with such merits of his own, should be without some distinctive name, and he strove to adapt it so as to indicate what he had been before belonging to a knight-errant, and what he then was; for it was only reasonable that, his master taking a new character, he should take a new name, and that it should be a distinguished and full-sounding one, befitting the new order and calling he was about to follow. And so, after having composed, struck out, rejected, added to, unmade, and remade a multitude of names out of his memory and fancy, he decided upon calling him Rocinante, a name, to his thinking, lofty, sonorous, and significant of his condition as a hack before he became what he now was, the first and foremost of all the hacks in the world.

Having got a name for his horse so much to his taste, he was anxious to get one for himself, and he was eight days more pondering over this point, till at last he made up his mind to call himself "Don Quixote," whence, as has been already said, the authors of this veracious history have inferred that his name must have been beyond a doubt Quixada, and not Quesada as others would have it. Recollecting, however, that the valiant Amadis was not content to call himself curtly Amadis and nothing more, but added the name of his kingdom and country to make it famous, and called himself Amadis of Gaul, he, like a good knight, resolved to add on the name of his, and to style himself Don Quixote of La Mancha, whereby, he considered, he described accurately his origin and country, and did honour to it in taking his surname from it.

So then, his armour being furbished, his morion turned into a helmet, his hack christened, and he himself confirmed, he came to the conclusion that nothing more was needed now but to look out for a lady to be in love with; for a knight-errant without love was like a tree without leaves or fruit, or a body without a soul. As he said to himself, "If, for my sins, or by my good fortune, I come across some giant hereabouts, a common occurrence with knights-errant, and overthrow him in one onslaught, or cleave him asunder to the waist, or, in short, vanquish and subdue him, will it not be well to have some one I may send him to as a present, that he may come in and fall on his knees before my sweet lady, and in a humble, submissive voice say, 'I am the giant Caraculiambro, lord of the island of Malindrania, vanquished in single combat by the never sufficiently extolled knight Don Quixote of La Mancha, who has commanded me to present myself before your Grace, that your Highness dispose of me at your pleasure'?" Oh, how our good gentleman enjoyed the delivery of this speech, especially when he had thought of some one to call his Lady! There was, so the story goes, in a village near his own a very good-looking farm-girl with whom he had been at one time in love, though, so far as is known, she never knew it nor gave a thought to the matter. Her name was Aldonza Lorenzo, and upon her he thought fit to confer the title of Lady of his Thoughts; and after some search for a name which should not be out of harmony with her own, and should suggest and indicate that of a princess and great lady, he decided upon calling her Dulcinea del Toboso—she being of El Toboso—a name, to his mind, musical, uncommon, and significant, like all those he had already bestowed upon himself and the things belonging to him.

CHAPTER II.

WHICH TREATS OF THE FIRST SALLY THE INGENIOUS DON QUIXOTE MADE FROM HOME

These preliminaries settled, he did not care to put off any longer the execution of his design, urged on to it by the thought of all the world was losing by his delay, seeing what wrongs he intended to right, grievances to redress, injustices to repair, abuses to remove, and duties to discharge. So, without giving notice of his intention to anyone, and without anybody seeing him, one morning before the dawning of the day (which was one of the hottest of the month of July) he donned his suit of armour, mounted Rocinante with his patched-up helmet on, braced his buckler, took his lance, and by the back door of the yard sallied forth upon the plain in the highest contentment and satisfaction at seeing with what ease he had made a beginning with his grand purpose. But scarcely did he find himself upon the open plain, when a terrible thought struck him, one all but enough to make him abandon the enterprise at the very outset. It occurred to him that he had not been dubbed a knight, and that according to the law of chivalry he neither could nor ought to bear arms against any knight; and that even if he had been, still he ought, as a novice knight, to wear white armour, without a device upon the shield until by his prowess he had earned one. These reflections made him waver in his purpose, but his craze being stronger than any reasoning, he made up his mind to have himself dubbed a knight by the first one he came across, following the example of others in the same case, as he had read in the books that brought him to this pass. As for white armour, he resolved, on the first opportunity, to scour his until it was whiter than an ermine; and so comforting himself he pursued his way, taking that which his horse chose, for in this he believed lay the essence of adventures.

Thus setting out, our new-fledged adventurer paced along, talking to himself and saying, "Who knows but that in time to come, when the veracious history of my famous deeds is made known, the sage who writes it, when he has to set forth my first sally in the early morning, will do it after this fashion? 'Scarce had the rubicund Apollo spread o'er the face of the broad spacious earth the golden threads of his bright hair, scarce had the little birds of painted plumage attuned their notes to hail with dulcet and mellifluous harmony the coming of the rosy Dawn, that, deserting the soft couch of her jealous spouse, was appearing to mortals at the gates and balconies of the Manchegan horizon, when the renowned knight Don Quixote of La Mancha, quitting the lazy down, mounted his celebrated steed Rocinante and began to traverse the ancient and famous Campo de Montiel;'" which in fact he was actually traversing. "Happy the age, happy the time," he continued, "in which shall be made known my deeds of fame, worthy to be moulded in brass, carved in marble, limned in pictures, for a memorial for ever. And thou, O sage magician, whoever thou art, to whom it shall fall to be the chronicler of this wondrous history, forget not, I entreat thee, my good Rocinante, the constant companion of my ways and wanderings." Presently he broke out again, as if he were love-stricken in earnest, "O Princess Dulcinea, lady of this captive heart, a grievous wrong hast thou done me to drive me forth with scorn, and with inexorable obduracy banish me from the presence of thy beauty. O lady, deign to hold in remembrance this heart, thy vassal, that thus in anguish pines for love of thee."

So he went on stringing together these and other absurdities, all in the style of those his books had taught him, imitating their language as well as he could; and all the while he rode so slowly and the sun mounted so rapidly and with such fervour that it was enough to melt his brains if he had any. Nearly all day he travelled without anything remarkable happening to him, at which he was in despair, for he was anxious to encounter some one at once upon whom to try the might of his strong arm.

Writers there are who say the first adventure he met with was that of Puerto Lapice; others say it was that of the windmills; but what I have ascertained on this point, and what I have found written in the annals of La Mancha, is that he was on the road all day, and towards nightfall his hack and he found themselves dead tired and hungry, when, looking all around to see if he could discover any castle or shepherd's shanty where he might refresh himself and relieve his sore wants, he perceived not far out of his road an inn, which was as welcome as a star guiding him to the portals, if not the palaces, of his redemption; and quickening his pace he reached it just as night was setting in. At the door were standing two young women, girls of the district as they call them, on their way to Seville with some carriers who had chanced to halt that night at the inn; and as, happen what might to our adventurer, everything he saw or imaged seemed to him to be and to happen after the fashion of what he read of, the moment he saw the inn he pictured it to himself as a castle with its four turrets and pinnacles of shining silver, not forgetting the drawbridge and moat and all the belongings usually ascribed to castles of the sort. To this inn, which to him seemed a castle, he advanced, and at a short distance from it he checked Rocinante, hoping that some dwarf would show himself upon the battlements, and by sound of trumpet give notice that a knight was approaching the castle. But seeing that they were slow about it, and that Rocinante was in a hurry to reach the stable, he made for the inn door, and perceived the two gay damsels who were standing there, and who seemed to him to be two fair maidens or lovely ladies taking their ease at the castle gate.

At this moment it so happened that a swineherd who was going through the stubbles collecting a drove of pigs (for, without any apology, that is what they are called) gave a blast of his horn to bring them together, and forthwith it seemed to Don Quixote to be what he was expecting, the signal of some dwarf announcing his arrival; and so with prodigious satisfaction he rode up to the inn and to the ladies, who, seeing a man of this sort approaching in full armour and with lance and buckler, were turning in dismay into the inn, when Don Quixote, guessing their fear by their flight, raising his pasteboard visor, disclosed his dry dusty visage, and with courteous bearing and gentle voice addressed them, "Your ladyships need not fly or fear any rudeness, for that it belongs not to the order of knighthood which I profess to offer to anyone, much less to highborn maidens as your appearance proclaims you to be." The girls were looking at him and straining their eyes to make out the features which the clumsy visor obscured, but when they heard themselves called maidens, a thing so much out of their line, they could not restrain their laughter, which made Don Quixote wax indignant, and say, "Modesty becomes the fair, and moreover laughter that has little cause is great silliness; this, however, I say not to pain or anger you, for my desire is none other than to serve you."

The incomprehensible language and the unpromising looks of our cavalier only increased the ladies' laughter, and that increased his irritation, and matters might have gone farther if at that moment the landlord had not come out, who, being a very fat man, was a very peaceful one. He, seeing this grotesque figure clad in armour that did not match any more than his saddle, bridle, lance, buckler, or corselet, was not at all indisposed to join the damsels in their manifestations of amusement; but, in truth, standing in awe of such a complicated armament, he thought it best to speak him fairly, so he said, "Senor Caballero, if your worship wants lodging, bating the bed (for there is not one in the inn) there is plenty of everything else here." Don Quixote, observing the respectful bearing of the Alcaide of the fortress (for so innkeeper and inn seemed in his eyes), made answer, "Sir Castellan, for me anything will suffice, for

'My armour is my only wear,

My only rest the fray.'"

The host fancied he called him Castellan because he took him for a "worthy of Castile," though he was in fact an Andalusian, and one from the strand of San Lucar, as crafty a thief as Cacus and as full of tricks as a student or a page. "In that case," said he,

"'Your bed is on the flinty rock,

Your sleep to watch alway;'

and if so, you may dismount and safely reckon upon any quantity of sleeplessness under this roof for a twelvemonth, not to say for a single night." So saying, he advanced to hold the stirrup for Don Quixote, who got down with great difficulty and exertion (for he had not broken his fast all day), and then charged the host to take great care of his horse, as he was the best bit of flesh that ever ate bread in this world. The landlord eyed him over but did not find him as good as Don Quixote said, nor even half as good; and putting him up in the stable, he returned to see what might be wanted by his guest, whom the damsels, who had by this time made their peace with him, were now relieving of his armour. They had taken off his breastplate and backpiece, but they neither knew nor saw how to open his gorget or remove his make-shift helmet, for he had fastened it with green ribbons, which, as there was no untying the knots, required to be cut. This, however, he would not by any means consent to, so he remained all the evening with his helmet on, the drollest and oddest figure that can be imagined; and while they were removing his armour, taking the baggages who were about it for ladies of high degree belonging to the castle, he said to them with great sprightliness:

"Oh, never, surely, was there knight

　So served by hand of dame,

As served was he, Don Quixote hight,

　When from his town he came;

With maidens waiting on himself,

　Princesses on his hack—

or Rocinante, for that, ladies mine, is my horse's name, and Don Quixote of La Mancha is my own; for though I had no intention of declaring myself until my achievements in your service and honour had made me known, the necessity of adapting that old ballad of Lancelot to the present occasion has given you the knowledge of my name altogether prematurely. A time, however, will come for your ladyships to command and me to obey, and then the might of my arm will show my desire to serve you."

The girls, who were not used to hearing rhetoric of this sort, had nothing to say in reply; they only asked him if he wanted anything to eat. "I would gladly eat a bit of something," said Don Quixote, "for I feel it would come very seasonably." The day happened to be a Friday, and in the whole inn there was nothing but some pieces of the fish they call in Castile "abadejo," in Andalusia "bacallao," and in some places "curadillo," and in others "troutlet;" so they asked him if he thought he could eat troutlet, for there was no other fish to give him. "If there be troutlets enough," said Don Quixote, "they will be the same thing as a trout; for it is all one to me whether I am given eight reals in small change or a piece of eight; moreover, it may be that these troutlets are like veal, which is better than beef, or kid, which is better than goat. But whatever it be let it come quickly, for the burden and pressure of arms cannot be borne without support to the inside." They laid a table for him at the door of the inn for the sake of the air, and the host brought him a portion of ill-soaked and worse cooked stockfish, and a piece of bread as black and mouldy as his own armour; but a laughable sight it was to see him eating, for having his helmet on and the beaver up, he could not with his own hands put anything into his mouth unless some one else placed it there, and this service one of the ladies rendered him. But to give him anything to drink was impossible, or would have been so had not the landlord bored a reed, and putting one end in his mouth poured the wine into him through the other; all which he bore with patience rather than sever the ribbons of his helmet.

While this was going on there came up to the inn a sowgelder, who, as he approached, sounded his reed pipe four or five times, and thereby completely convinced Don Quixote that he was in some famous castle, and that they were regaling him with music, and that the stockfish was trout, the bread the whitest, the wenches ladies, and the landlord the castellan of the castle; and consequently he held that his enterprise and sally had been to some purpose. But still it distressed him to think he had not been dubbed a knight, for it was plain to him he could not lawfully engage in any adventure without receiving the order of knighthood.

CHAPTER III.

WHEREIN IS RELATED THE DROLL WAY IN WHICH DON QUIXOTE HAD HIMSELF DUBBED A KNIGHT

Harassed by this reflection, he made haste with his scanty pothouse supper, and having finished it called the landlord, and shutting himself into the stable with him, fell on his knees before him, saying, "From this spot I rise not, valiant knight, until your courtesy grants me the boon I seek, one that will redound to your praise and the benefit of the human race." The landlord, seeing his guest at his feet and hearing a speech of this kind, stood staring at him in bewilderment, not knowing what to do or say, and entreating him to rise, but all to no purpose until he had agreed to grant the boon demanded of him. "I looked for no less, my lord, from your High Magnificence," replied Don Quixote, "and I have to tell you that the boon I have asked and your liberality has granted is that you shall dub me knight to-morrow morning, and that to-night I shall watch my arms in the chapel of this your castle; thus tomorrow, as I have said, will be accomplished what I so much desire, enabling me lawfully to roam through all the four quarters of the world seeking adventures on behalf of those in distress, as is the duty of chivalry and of knights-errant like myself, whose ambition is directed to such deeds."

The landlord, who, as has been mentioned, was something of a wag, and had already some suspicion of his guest's want of wits, was quite convinced of it on hearing talk of this kind from him, and to make sport for the night he determined to fall in with his humour. So he told him he was quite right in pursuing the object he had in view, and that such a motive was natural and becoming in cavaliers as distinguished as he seemed and his gallant bearing showed him to be; and that he himself in his younger days had followed the same honourable calling, roaming in quest of adventures in various parts of the world, among others the Curing-grounds of Malaga, the Isles of Riaran, the Precinct of Seville, the Little Market of Segovia, the Olivera of Valencia, the Rondilla of Granada, the Strand of San Lucar, the Colt of Cordova, the Taverns of Toledo, and divers other quarters, where he had proved the nimbleness of his feet and the lightness of his fingers, doing many wrongs, cheating many widows, ruining maids and swindling minors, and, in short, bringing himself under the notice of almost every tribunal and court of justice in Spain; until at last he had retired to this castle of his, where he was living upon his property and upon that of others; and where he received all knights-errant of whatever rank or condition they might be, all for the great love he bore them and that they might share their substance with him in return for his benevolence. He told him, moreover, that in this castle of his there was no chapel in which he could watch his armour, as it had been pulled down in order to be rebuilt, but that in a case of necessity it might, he knew, be watched anywhere, and he might watch it that night in a courtyard of the castle, and in the morning, God willing, the requisite ceremonies might be performed so as to have him dubbed a knight, and so thoroughly dubbed that nobody could be more so. He asked if he had any money with him, to which Don Quixote replied that he had not a farthing, as in the histories of knights-errant he had never read of any of them carrying any. On this point the landlord told him he was mistaken; for, though not recorded in the histories, because in the author's opinion there was no need to mention anything so obvious and necessary as money and clean shirts, it was not to be supposed therefore that they did not carry them, and he might regard it as certain and established that all knights-errant (about whom there were so many full and unimpeachable books) carried well-furnished purses in case of emergency, and likewise carried shirts and a little box of ointment to cure the wounds they received. For in those plains and deserts where they engaged in combat and came out wounded, it was not always that there was some one to cure them, unless indeed they had for a friend some sage magician to succour them at once by fetching through the air upon a cloud some damsel or dwarf with a vial of water of such virtue that by tasting one drop of it they were cured of their hurts and wounds in an instant and left as sound as if they had not received any damage whatever. But in case this should not occur, the knights of old took care to see that their squires were provided with money and other requisites, such as lint and ointments for healing purposes; and when it happened that knights had no squires (which was rarely and seldom the case) they themselves carried everything in cunning saddle-bags that were hardly seen on the horse's croup, as if it were something else of more importance, because, unless for some such reason, carrying saddle-bags was not very favourably regarded among knights-errant. He therefore advised him (and, as his godson so soon to be, he might even command him) never from that time forth to travel without money and the usual requirements, and he would find the advantage of them when he least expected it.

Don Quixote promised to follow his advice scrupulously, and it was arranged forthwith that he should watch his armour in a large yard at one side of the inn; so, collecting it all together, Don Quixote placed it on a trough that stood by the side of a well, and bracing his buckler on his arm he grasped his lance and began with a stately air to march up and down in front of the trough, and as he began his march night began to fall.

The landlord told all the people who were in the inn about the craze of his guest, the watching of the armour, and the dubbing ceremony he contemplated. Full of wonder at so strange a form of madness, they flocked to see it from a distance, and observed with what composure he sometimes paced up and down, or sometimes, leaning on his lance, gazed on his armour without taking his eyes off it for ever so long; and as the night closed in with a light from the moon so brilliant that it might vie with his that lent it, everything the novice knight did was plainly seen by all.

Meanwhile one of the carriers who were in the inn thought fit to water his team, and it was necessary to remove Don Quixote's armour as it lay on the trough; but he seeing the other approach hailed him in a loud voice, "O thou, whoever thou art, rash knight that comest to lay hands on the armour of the most valorous errant that ever girt on sword, have a care what thou dost; touch it not unless thou wouldst lay down thy life as the penalty of thy rashness." The carrier gave no heed to these words (and he would have done better to heed them if he had been heedful of his health), but seizing it by the straps flung the armour some distance from him. Seeing this, Don Quixote raised his eyes to heaven, and fixing his thoughts, apparently, upon his lady Dulcinea, exclaimed, "Aid me, lady mine, in this the first encounter that presents itself to this breast which thou holdest in subjection; let not thy favour and protection fail me in this first jeopardy;" and, with these words and others to the same purpose, dropping his buckler he lifted his lance with both hands and with it smote such a blow on the carrier's head that he stretched him on the ground, so stunned that had he followed it up with a second there would have been no need of a surgeon to cure him. This done, he picked up his armour and returned to his beat with the same serenity as before.

Shortly after this, another, not knowing what had happened (for the carrier still lay senseless), came with the same object of giving water to his mules, and was proceeding to remove the armour in order to clear the trough, when Don Quixote, without uttering a word or imploring aid from anyone, once more dropped his buckler and once more lifted his lance, and without actually breaking the second carrier's head into pieces, made more than three of it, for he laid it open in four. At the noise all the people of the inn ran to the spot, and among them the landlord. Seeing this, Don Quixote braced his buckler on his arm, and with his hand on his sword exclaimed, "O Lady of Beauty, strength and support of my faint heart, it is time for thee to turn the eyes of thy greatness on this thy captive knight on the brink of so mighty an adventure." By this he felt himself so inspired that he would not have flinched if all the carriers in the world had assailed him. The comrades of the wounded perceiving the plight they were in began from a distance to shower stones on Don Quixote, who screened himself as best he could with his buckler, not daring to quit the trough and leave his armour unprotected. The landlord shouted to them to leave him alone, for he had already told them that he was mad, and as a madman he would not be accountable even if he killed them all. Still louder shouted Don Quixote, calling them knaves and traitors, and the lord of the castle, who allowed knights-errant to be treated in this fashion, a villain and a low-born knight whom, had he received the order of knighthood, he would call to account for his treachery. "But of you," he cried, "base and vile rabble, I make no account; fling, strike, come on, do all ye can against me, ye shall see what the reward of your folly and insolence will be." This he uttered with so much spirit and boldness that he filled his assailants with a terrible fear, and as much for this reason as at the persuasion of the landlord they left off stoning him, and he allowed them to carry off the wounded, and with the same calmness and composure as before resumed the watch over his armour.

But these freaks of his guest were not much to the liking of the landlord, so he determined to cut matters short and confer upon him at once the unlucky order of knighthood before any further misadventure could occur; so, going up to him, he apologised for the rudeness which, without his knowledge, had been offered to him by these low people, who, however, had been well punished for their audacity. As he had already told him, he said, there was no chapel in the castle, nor was it needed for what remained to be done, for, as he understood the ceremonial of the order, the whole point of being dubbed a knight lay in the accolade and in the slap on the shoulder, and that could be administered in the middle of a field; and that he had now done all that was needful as to watching the armour, for all requirements were satisfied by a watch of two hours only, while he had been more than four about it. Don Quixote believed it all, and told him he stood there ready to obey him, and to make an end of it with as much despatch as possible; for, if he were again attacked, and felt himself to be dubbed knight, he would not, he thought, leave a soul alive in the castle, except such as out of respect he might spare at his bidding.

Thus warned and menaced, the castellan forthwith brought out a book in which he used to enter the straw and barley he served out to the carriers, and, with a lad carrying a candle-end, and the two damsels already mentioned, he returned to where Don Quixote stood, and bade him kneel down. Then, reading from his account-book as if he were repeating some devout prayer, in the middle of his delivery he raised his hand and gave him a sturdy blow on the neck, and then, with his own sword, a smart slap on the shoulder, all the while muttering between his teeth as if he was saying his prayers. Having done this, he directed one of the ladies to gird on his sword, which she did with great self-possession and gravity, and not a little was required to prevent a burst of laughter at each stage of the ceremony; but what they had already seen of the novice knight's prowess kept their laughter within bounds. On girding him with the sword the worthy lady said to him, "May God make your worship a very fortunate knight, and grant you success in battle." Don Quixote asked her name in order that he might from that time forward know to whom he was beholden for the favour he had received, as he meant to confer upon her some portion of the honour he acquired by the might of his arm. She answered with great humility that she was called La Tolosa, and that she was the daughter of a cobbler of Toledo who lived in the stalls of Sanchobienaya, and that wherever she might be she would serve and esteem him as her lord. Don Quixote said in reply that she would do him a favour if thenceforward she assumed the "Don" and called herself Dona Tolosa. She promised she would, and then the other buckled on his spur, and with her followed almost the same conversation as with the lady of the sword. He asked her name, and she said it was La Molinera, and that she was the daughter of a respectable miller of Antequera; and of her likewise Don Quixote requested that she would adopt the "Don" and call herself Dona Molinera, making offers to her further services and favours.

Having thus, with hot haste and speed, brought to a conclusion these never-till-now-seen ceremonies, Don Quixote was on thorns until he saw himself on horseback sallying forth in quest of adventures; and saddling Rocinante at once he mounted, and embracing his host, as he returned thanks for his kindness in knighting him, he addressed him in language so extraordinary that it is impossible to convey an idea of it or report it. The landlord, to get him out of the inn, replied with no less rhetoric though with shorter words, and without calling upon him to pay the reckoning let him go with a Godspeed.

CHAPTER IV.

OF WHAT HAPPENED TO OUR KNIGHT WHEN HE LEFT THE INN

Day was dawning when Don Quixote quitted the inn, so happy, so gay, so exhilarated at finding himself now dubbed a knight, that his joy was like to burst his horse-girths. However, recalling the advice of his host as to the requisites he ought to carry with him, especially that referring to money and shirts, he determined to go home and provide himself with all, and also with a squire, for he reckoned upon securing a farm-labourer, a neighbour of his, a poor man with a family, but very well qualified for the office of squire to a knight. With this object he turned his horse's head towards his village, and Rocinante, thus reminded of his old quarters, stepped out so briskly that he hardly seemed to tread the earth.

He had not gone far, when out of a thicket on his right there seemed to come feeble cries as of some one in distress, and the instant he heard them he exclaimed, "Thanks be to heaven for the favour it accords me, that it so soon offers me an opportunity of fulfilling the obligation I have undertaken, and gathering the fruit of my ambition. These cries, no doubt, come from some man or woman in want of help, and needing my aid and protection;" and wheeling, he turned Rocinante in the direction whence the cries seemed to proceed. He had gone but a few paces into the wood, when he saw a mare tied to an oak, and tied to another, and stripped from the waist upwards, a youth of about fifteen years of age, from whom the cries came. Nor were they without cause, for a lusty farmer was flogging him with a belt and following up every blow with scoldings and commands, repeating, "Your mouth shut and your eyes open!" while the youth made answer, "I won't do it again, master mine; by God's passion I won't do it again, and I'll take more care of the flock another time."

Seeing what was going on, Don Quixote said in an angry voice, "Discourteous knight, it ill becomes you to assail one who cannot defend himself; mount your steed and take your lance" (for there was a lance leaning against the oak to which the mare was tied), "and I will make you know that you are behaving as a coward." The farmer, seeing before him this figure in full armour brandishing a lance over his head, gave himself up for dead, and made answer meekly, "Sir Knight, this youth that I am chastising is my servant, employed by me to watch a flock of sheep that I have hard by, and he is so careless that I lose one every day, and when I punish him for his carelessness and knavery he says I do it out of niggardliness, to escape paying him the wages I owe him, and before God, and on my soul, he lies."

"Lies before me, base clown!" said Don Quixote. "By the sun that shines on us I have a mind to run you through with this lance. Pay him at once without another word; if not, by the God that rules us I will make an end of you, and annihilate you on the spot; release him instantly."

The farmer hung his head, and without a word untied his servant, of whom

Don Quixote asked how much his master owed him.

He replied, nine months at seven reals a month. Don Quixote added it up, found that it came to sixty-three reals, and told the farmer to pay it down immediately, if he did not want to die for it.

The trembling clown replied that as he lived and by the oath he had sworn (though he had not sworn any) it was not so much; for there were to be taken into account and deducted three pairs of shoes he had given him, and a real for two blood-lettings when he was sick.

"All that is very well," said Don Quixote; "but let the shoes and the blood-lettings stand as a setoff against the blows you have given him without any cause; for if he spoiled the leather of the shoes you paid for, you have damaged that of his body, and if the barber took blood from him when he was sick, you have drawn it when he was sound; so on that score he owes you nothing."

"The difficulty is, Sir Knight, that I have no money here; let Andres come home with me, and I will pay him all, real by real."

"I go with him!" said the youth. "Nay, God forbid! No, senor, not for the world; for once alone with me, he would ray me like a Saint Bartholomew."

"He will do nothing of the kind," said Don Quixote; "I have only to command, and he will obey me; and as he has sworn to me by the order of knighthood which he has received, I leave him free, and I guarantee the payment."

"Consider what you are saying, senor," said the youth; "this master of mine is not a knight, nor has he received any order of knighthood; for he is Juan Haldudo the Rich, of Quintanar."

"That matters little," replied Don Quixote; "there may be Haldudos knights; moreover, everyone is the son of his works."

"That is true," said Andres; "but this master of mine—of what works is he the son, when he refuses me the wages of my sweat and labour?"

"I do not refuse, brother Andres," said the farmer, "be good enough to come along with me, and I swear by all the orders of knighthood there are in the world to pay you as I have agreed, real by real, and perfumed."

"For the perfumery I excuse you," said Don Quixote; "give it to him in reals, and I shall be satisfied; and see that you do as you have sworn; if not, by the same oath I swear to come back and hunt you out and punish you; and I shall find you though you should lie closer than a lizard. And if you desire to know who it is lays this command upon you, that you be more firmly bound to obey it, know that I am the valorous Don Quixote of La Mancha, the undoer of wrongs and injustices; and so, God be with you, and keep in mind what you have promised and sworn under those penalties that have been already declared to you."

So saying, he gave Rocinante the spur and was soon out of reach. The farmer followed him with his eyes, and when he saw that he had cleared the wood and was no longer in sight, he turned to his boy Andres, and said, "Come here, my son, I want to pay you what I owe you, as that undoer of wrongs has commanded me."

"My oath on it," said Andres, "your worship will be well advised to obey the command of that good knight—may he live a thousand years—for, as he is a valiant and just judge, by Roque, if you do not pay me, he will come back and do as he said."

"My oath on it, too," said the farmer; "but as I have a strong affection for you, I want to add to the debt in order to add to the payment;" and seizing him by the arm, he tied him up again, and gave him such a flogging that he left him for dead.

"Now, Master Andres," said the farmer, "call on the undoer of wrongs; you will find he won't undo that, though I am not sure that I have quite done with you, for I have a good mind to flay you alive." But at last he untied him, and gave him leave to go look for his judge in order to put the sentence pronounced into execution.

Andres went off rather down in the mouth, swearing he would go to look for the valiant Don Quixote of La Mancha and tell him exactly what had happened, and that all would have to be repaid him sevenfold; but for all that, he went off weeping, while his master stood laughing.

Thus did the valiant Don Quixote right that wrong, and, thoroughly satisfied with what had taken place, as he considered he had made a very happy and noble beginning with his knighthood, he took the road towards his village in perfect self-content, saying in a low voice, "Well mayest thou this day call thyself fortunate above all on earth, O Dulcinea del Toboso, fairest of the fair! since it has fallen to thy lot to hold subject and submissive to thy full will and pleasure a knight so renowned as is and will be Don Quixote of La Mancha, who, as all the world knows, yesterday received the order of knighthood, and hath to-day righted the greatest wrong and grievance that ever injustice conceived and cruelty perpetrated: who hath to-day plucked the rod from the hand of yonder ruthless oppressor so wantonly lashing that tender child."

He now came to a road branching in four directions, and immediately he was reminded of those cross-roads where knights-errant used to stop to consider which road they should take. In imitation of them he halted for a while, and after having deeply considered it, he gave Rocinante his head, submitting his own will to that of his hack, who followed out his first intention, which was to make straight for his own stable. After he had gone about two miles Don Quixote perceived a large party of people, who, as afterwards appeared, were some Toledo traders, on their way to buy silk at Murcia. There were six of them coming along under their sunshades, with four servants mounted, and three muleteers on foot. Scarcely had Don Quixote descried them when the fancy possessed him that this must be some new adventure; and to help him to imitate as far as he could those passages he had read of in his books, here seemed to come one made on purpose, which he resolved to attempt. So with a lofty bearing and determination he fixed himself firmly in his stirrups, got his lance ready, brought his buckler before his breast, and planting himself in the middle of the road, stood waiting the approach of these knights-errant, for such he now considered and held them to be; and when they had come near enough to see and hear, he exclaimed with a haughty gesture, "All the world stand, unless all the world confess that in all the world there is no maiden fairer than the Empress of La Mancha, the peerless Dulcinea del Toboso."

The traders halted at the sound of this language and the sight of the strange figure that uttered it, and from both figure and language at once guessed the craze of their owner; they wished, however, to learn quietly what was the object of this confession that was demanded of them, and one of them, who was rather fond of a joke and was very sharp-witted, said to him, "Sir Knight, we do not know who this good lady is that you speak of; show her to us, for, if she be of such beauty as you suggest, with all our hearts and without any pressure we will confess the truth that is on your part required of us."

"If I were to show her to you," replied Don Quixote, "what merit would you have in confessing a truth so manifest? The essential point is that without seeing her you must believe, confess, affirm, swear, and defend it; else ye have to do with me in battle, ill-conditioned, arrogant rabble that ye are; and come ye on, one by one as the order of knighthood requires, or all together as is the custom and vile usage of your breed, here do I bide and await you relying on the justice of the cause I maintain."

"Sir Knight," replied the trader, "I entreat your worship in the name of this present company of princes, that, to save us from charging our consciences with the confession of a thing we have never seen or heard of, and one moreover so much to the prejudice of the Empresses and Queens of the Alcarria and Estremadura, your worship will be pleased to show us some portrait of this lady, though it be no bigger than a grain of wheat; for by the thread one gets at the ball, and in this way we shall be satisfied and easy, and you will be content and pleased; nay, I believe we are already so far agreed with you that even though her portrait should show her blind of one eye, and distilling vermilion and sulphur from the other, we would nevertheless, to gratify your worship, say all in her favour that you desire."

"She distils nothing of the kind, vile rabble," said Don Quixote, burning with rage, "nothing of the kind, I say, only ambergris and civet in cotton; nor is she one-eyed or humpbacked, but straighter than a Guadarrama spindle: but ye must pay for the blasphemy ye have uttered against beauty like that of my lady."

And so saying, he charged with levelled lance against the one who had spoken, with such fury and fierceness that, if luck had not contrived that Rocinante should stumble midway and come down, it would have gone hard with the rash trader. Down went Rocinante, and over went his master, rolling along the ground for some distance; and when he tried to rise he was unable, so encumbered was he with lance, buckler, spurs, helmet, and the weight of his old armour; and all the while he was struggling to get up he kept saying, "Fly not, cowards and caitiffs! stay, for not by my fault, but my horse's, am I stretched here."

One of the muleteers in attendance, who could not have had much good nature in him, hearing the poor prostrate man blustering in this style, was unable to refrain from giving him an answer on his ribs; and coming up to him he seized his lance, and having broken it in pieces, with one of them he began so to belabour our Don Quixote that, notwithstanding and in spite of his armour, he milled him like a measure of wheat. His masters called out not to lay on so hard and to leave him alone, but the muleteers blood was up, and he did not care to drop the game until he had vented the rest of his wrath, and gathering up the remaining fragments of the lance he finished with a discharge upon the unhappy victim, who all through the storm of sticks that rained on him never ceased threatening heaven, and earth, and the brigands, for such they seemed to him. At last the muleteer was tired, and the traders continued their journey, taking with them matter for talk about the poor fellow who had been cudgelled. He when he found himself alone made another effort to rise; but if he was unable when whole and sound, how was he to rise after having been thrashed and well-nigh knocked to pieces? And yet he esteemed himself fortunate, as it seemed to him that this was a regular knight-errant's mishap, and entirely, he considered, the fault of his horse. However, battered in body as he was, to rise was beyond his power.

CHAPTER V.

IN WHICH THE NARRATIVE OF OUR KNIGHT'S MISHAP IS CONTINUED

Finding, then, that, in fact he could not move, he thought himself of having recourse to his usual remedy, which was to think of some passage in his books, and his craze brought to his mind that about Baldwin and the Marquis of Mantua, when Carloto left him wounded on the mountain side, a story known by heart by the children, not forgotten by the young men, and lauded and even believed by the old folk; and for all that not a whit truer than the miracles of Mahomet. This seemed to him to fit exactly the case in which he found himself, so, making a show of severe suffering, he began to roll on the ground and with feeble breath repeat the very words which the wounded knight of the wood is said to have uttered:

Where art thou, lady mine, that thou

  My sorrow dost not rue?

Thou canst not know it, lady mine,

  Or else thou art untrue.

And so he went on with the ballad as far as the lines:

O noble Marquis of Mantua,

  My Uncle and liege lord!

As chance would have it, when he had got to this line there happened to come by a peasant from his own village, a neighbour of his, who had been with a load of wheat to the mill, and he, seeing the man stretched there, came up to him and asked him who he was and what was the matter with him that he complained so dolefully.

Don Quixote was firmly persuaded that this was the Marquis of Mantua, his uncle, so the only answer he made was to go on with his ballad, in which he told the tale of his misfortune, and of the loves of the Emperor's son and his wife all exactly as the ballad sings it.

The peasant stood amazed at hearing such nonsense, and relieving him of the visor, already battered to pieces by blows, he wiped his face, which was covered with dust, and as soon as he had done so he recognised him and said, "Senor Quixada" (for so he appears to have been called when he was in his senses and had not yet changed from a quiet country gentleman into a knight-errant), "who has brought your worship to this pass?" But to all questions the other only went on with his ballad.

Seeing this, the good man removed as well as he could his breastplate and backpiece to see if he had any wound, but he could perceive no blood nor any mark whatever. He then contrived to raise him from the ground, and with no little difficulty hoisted him upon his ass, which seemed to him to be the easiest mount for him; and collecting the arms, even to the splinters of the lance, he tied them on Rocinante, and leading him by the bridle and the ass by the halter he took the road for the village, very sad to hear what absurd stuff Don Quixote was talking.

Nor was Don Quixote less so, for what with blows and bruises he could not sit upright on the ass, and from time to time he sent up sighs to heaven, so that once more he drove the peasant to ask what ailed him. And it could have been only the devil himself that put into his head tales to match his own adventures, for now, forgetting Baldwin, he bethought himself of the Moor Abindarraez, when the Alcaide of Antequera, Rodrigo de Narvaez, took him prisoner and carried him away to his castle; so that when the peasant again asked him how he was and what ailed him, he gave him for reply the same words and phrases that the captive Abindarraez gave to Rodrigo de Narvaez, just as he had read the story in the "Diana" of Jorge de Montemayor where it is written, applying it to his own case so aptly that the peasant went along cursing his fate that he had to listen to such a lot of nonsense; from which, however, he came to the conclusion that his neighbour was mad, and so made all haste to reach the village to escape the wearisomeness of this harangue of Don Quixote's; who, at the end of it, said, "Senor Don Rodrigo de Narvaez, your worship must know that this fair Xarifa I have mentioned is now the lovely Dulcinea del Toboso, for whom I have done, am doing, and will do the most famous deeds of chivalry that in this world have been seen, are to be seen, or ever shall be seen."

To this the peasant answered, "Senor—sinner that I am!—cannot your worship see that I am not Don Rodrigo de Narvaez nor the Marquis of

Mantua, but Pedro Alonso your neighbour, and that your worship is neither

Baldwin nor Abindarraez, but the worthy gentleman Senor Quixada?"

"I know who I am," replied Don Quixote, "and I know that I may be not only those I have named, but all the Twelve Peers of France and even all the Nine Worthies, since my achievements surpass all that they have done all together and each of them on his own account."

With this talk and more of the same kind they reached the village just as night was beginning to fall, but the peasant waited until it was a little later that the belaboured gentleman might not be seen riding in such a miserable trim. When it was what seemed to him the proper time he entered the village and went to Don Quixote's house, which he found all in confusion, and there were the curate and the village barber, who were great friends of Don Quixote, and his housekeeper was saying to them in a loud voice, "What does your worship think can have befallen my master, Senor Licentiate Pero Perez?" for so the curate was called; "it is three days now since anything has been seen of him, or the hack, or the buckler, lance, or armour. Miserable me! I am certain of it, and it is as true as that I was born to die, that these accursed books of chivalry he has, and has got into the way of reading so constantly, have upset his reason; for now I remember having often heard him saying to himself that he would turn knight-errant and go all over the world in quest of adventures. To the devil and Barabbas with such books, that have brought to ruin in this way the finest understanding there was in all La Mancha!"

The niece said the same, and, more: "You must know, Master Nicholas"—for that was the name of the barber—"it was often my uncle's way to stay two days and nights together poring over these unholy books of misventures, after which he would fling the book away and snatch up his sword and fall to slashing the walls; and when he was tired out he would say he had killed four giants like four towers; and the sweat that flowed from him when he was weary he said was the blood of the wounds he had received in battle; and then he would drink a great jug of cold water and become calm and quiet, saying that this water was a most precious potion which the sage Esquife, a great magician and friend of his, had brought him. But I take all the blame upon myself for never having told your worships of my uncle's vagaries, that you might put a stop to them before things had come to this pass, and burn all these accursed books—for he has a great number—that richly deserve to be burned like heretics."

"So say I too," said the curate, "and by my faith to-morrow shall not pass without public judgment upon them, and may they be condemned to the flames lest they lead those that read to behave as my good friend seems to have behaved."

All this the peasant heard, and from it he understood at last what was the matter with his neighbour, so he began calling aloud, "Open, your worships, to Senor Baldwin and to Senor the Marquis of Mantua, who comes badly wounded, and to Senor Abindarraez, the Moor, whom the valiant Rodrigo de Narvaez, the Alcaide of Antequera, brings captive."

At these words they all hurried out, and when they recognised their friend, master, and uncle, who had not yet dismounted from the ass because he could not, they ran to embrace him.

"Hold!" said he, "for I am badly wounded through my horse's fault; carry me to bed, and if possible send for the wise Urganda to cure and see to my wounds."

"See there! plague on it!" cried the housekeeper at this: "did not my heart tell the truth as to which foot my master went lame of? To bed with your worship at once, and we will contrive to cure you here without fetching that Hurgada. A curse I say once more, and a hundred times more, on those books of chivalry that have brought your worship to such a pass."

They carried him to bed at once, and after searching for his wounds could find none, but he said they were all bruises from having had a severe fall with his horse Rocinante when in combat with ten giants, the biggest and the boldest to be found on earth.

"So, so!" said the curate, "are there giants in the dance? By the sign of the Cross I will burn them to-morrow before the day over."

They put a host of questions to Don Quixote, but his only answer to all was—give him something to eat, and leave him to sleep, for that was what he needed most. They did so, and the curate questioned the peasant at great length as to how he had found Don Quixote. He told him, and the nonsense he had talked when found and on the way home, all which made the licentiate the more eager to do what he did the next day, which was to summon his friend the barber, Master Nicholas, and go with him to Don Quixote's house.

CHAPTER VI.

OF THE DIVERTING AND IMPORTANT SCRUTINY WHICH THE CURATE AND THE BARBER MADE IN THE LIBRARY OF OUR INGENIOUS GENTLEMAN

He was still sleeping; so the curate asked the niece for the keys of the room where the books, the authors of all the mischief, were, and right willingly she gave them. They all went in, the housekeeper with them, and found more than a hundred volumes of big books very well bound, and some other small ones. The moment the housekeeper saw them she turned about and ran out of the room, and came back immediately with a saucer of holy water and a sprinkler, saying, "Here, your worship, senor licentiate, sprinkle this room; don't leave any magician of the many there are in these books to bewitch us in revenge for our design of banishing them from the world."

The simplicity of the housekeeper made the licentiate laugh, and he directed the barber to give him the books one by one to see what they were about, as there might be some to be found among them that did not deserve the penalty of fire.

"No," said the niece, "there is no reason for showing mercy to any of them; they have every one of them done mischief; better fling them out of the window into the court and make a pile of them and set fire to them; or else carry them into the yard, and there a bonfire can be made without the smoke giving any annoyance." The housekeeper said the same, so eager were they both for the slaughter of those innocents, but the curate would not agree to it without first reading at any rate the titles.

The first that Master Nicholas put into his hand was "The four books of Amadis of Gaul." "This seems a mysterious thing," said the curate, "for, as I have heard say, this was the first book of chivalry printed in Spain, and from this all the others derive their birth and origin; so it seems to me that we ought inexorably to condemn it to the flames as the founder of so vile a sect."

"Nay, sir," said the barber, "I too, have heard say that this is the best of all the books of this kind that have been written, and so, as something singular in its line, it ought to be pardoned."

"True," said the curate; "and for that reason let its life be spared for the present. Let us see that other which is next to it."

"It is," said the barber, "the 'Sergas de Esplandian,' the lawful son of

Amadis of Gaul."

"Then verily," said the curate, "the merit of the father must not be put down to the account of the son. Take it, mistress housekeeper; open the window and fling it into the yard and lay the foundation of the pile for the bonfire we are to make."

The housekeeper obeyed with great satisfaction, and the worthy "Esplandian" went flying into the yard to await with all patience the fire that was in store for him.

"Proceed," said the curate.

"This that comes next," said the barber, "is 'Amadis of Greece,' and, indeed, I believe all those on this side are of the same Amadis lineage."

"Then to the yard with the whole of them," said the curate; "for to have the burning of Queen Pintiquiniestra, and the shepherd Darinel and his eclogues, and the bedevilled and involved discourses of his author, I would burn with them the father who begot me if he were going about in the guise of a knight-errant."

"I am of the same mind," said the barber.

"And so am I," added the niece.

"In that case," said the housekeeper, "here, into the yard with them!"

They were handed to her, and as there were many of them, she spared herself the staircase, and flung them down out of the window.

"Who is that tub there?" said the curate.

"This," said the barber, "is 'Don Olivante de Laura.'"

"The author of that book," said the curate, "was the same that wrote 'The Garden of Flowers,' and truly there is no deciding which of the two books is the more truthful, or, to put it better, the less lying; all I can say is, send this one into the yard for a swaggering fool."

"This that follows is 'Florismarte of Hircania,'" said the barber.

"Senor Florismarte here?" said the curate; "then by my faith he must take up his quarters in the yard, in spite of his marvellous birth and visionary adventures, for the stiffness and dryness of his style deserve nothing else; into the yard with him and the other, mistress housekeeper."

"With all my heart, senor," said she, and executed the order with great delight.

"This," said the barber, "is The Knight Platir.'"

"An old book that," said the curate, "but I find no reason for clemency in it; send it after the others without appeal;" which was done.

Another book was opened, and they saw it was entitled, "The Knight of the

Cross."

"For the sake of the holy name this book has," said the curate, "its ignorance might be excused; but then, they say, 'behind the cross there's the devil; to the fire with it."

Taking down another book, the barber said, "This is 'The Mirror of

Chivalry.'"

"I know his worship," said the curate; "that is where Senor Reinaldos of Montalvan figures with his friends and comrades, greater thieves than Cacus, and the Twelve Peers of France with the veracious historian Turpin; however, I am not for condemning them to more than perpetual banishment, because, at any rate, they have some share in the invention of the famous Matteo Boiardo, whence too the Christian poet Ludovico Ariosto wove his web, to whom, if I find him here, and speaking any language but his own, I shall show no respect whatever; but if he speaks his own tongue I will put him upon my head."

"Well, I have him in Italian," said the barber, "but I do not understand him."

"Nor would it be well that you should understand him," said the curate, "and on that score we might have excused the Captain if he had not brought him into Spain and turned him into Castilian. He robbed him of a great deal of his natural force, and so do all those who try to turn books written in verse into another language, for, with all the pains they take and all the cleverness they show, they never can reach the level of the originals as they were first produced. In short, I say that this book, and all that may be found treating of those French affairs, should be thrown into or deposited in some dry well, until after more consideration it is settled what is to be done with them; excepting always one 'Bernardo del Carpio' that is going about, and another called 'Roncesvalles;' for these, if they come into my hands, shall pass at once into those of the housekeeper, and from hers into the fire without any reprieve."

To all this the barber gave his assent, and looked upon it as right and proper, being persuaded that the curate was so staunch to the Faith and loyal to the Truth that he would not for the world say anything opposed to them. Opening another book he saw it was "Palmerin de Oliva," and beside it was another called "Palmerin of England," seeing which the licentiate said, "Let the Olive be made firewood of at once and burned until no ashes even are left; and let that Palm of England be kept and preserved as a thing that stands alone, and let such another case be made for it as that which Alexander found among the spoils of Darius and set aside for the safe keeping of the works of the poet Homer. This book, gossip, is of authority for two reasons, first because it is very good, and secondly because it is said to have been written by a wise and witty king of Portugal. All the adventures at the Castle of Miraguarda are excellent and of admirable contrivance, and the language is polished and clear, studying and observing the style befitting the speaker with propriety and judgment. So then, provided it seems good to you, Master Nicholas, I say let this and 'Amadis of Gaul' be remitted the penalty of fire, and as for all the rest, let them perish without further question or query."

"Nay, gossip," said the barber, "for this that I have here is the famous

'Don Belianis.'"

"Well," said the curate, "that and the second, third, and fourth parts all stand in need of a little rhubarb to purge their excess of bile, and they must be cleared of all that stuff about the Castle of Fame and other greater affectations, to which end let them be allowed the over-seas term, and, according as they mend, so shall mercy or justice be meted out to them; and in the mean time, gossip, do you keep them in your house and let no one read them."

"With all my heart," said the barber; and not caring to tire himself with reading more books of chivalry, he told the housekeeper to take all the big ones and throw them into the yard. It was not said to one dull or deaf, but to one who enjoyed burning them more than weaving the broadest and finest web that could be; and seizing about eight at a time, she flung them out of the window.

In carrying so many together she let one fall at the feet of the barber, who took it up, curious to know whose it was, and found it said, "History of the Famous Knight, Tirante el Blanco."

"God bless me!" said the curate with a shout, "'Tirante el Blanco' here! Hand it over, gossip, for in it I reckon I have found a treasury of enjoyment and a mine of recreation. Here is Don Kyrieleison of Montalvan, a valiant knight, and his brother Thomas of Montalvan, and the knight Fonseca, with the battle the bold Tirante fought with the mastiff, and the witticisms of the damsel Placerdemivida, and the loves and wiles of the widow Reposada, and the empress in love with the squire Hipolito—in truth, gossip, by right of its style it is the best book in the world. Here knights eat and sleep, and die in their beds, and make their wills before dying, and a great deal more of which there is nothing in all the other books. Nevertheless, I say he who wrote it, for deliberately composing such fooleries, deserves to be sent to the galleys for life. Take it home with you and read it, and you will see that what I have said is true."

"As you will," said the barber; "but what are we to do with these little books that are left?"

"These must be, not chivalry, but poetry," said the curate; and opening one he saw it was the "Diana" of Jorge de Montemayor, and, supposing all the others to be of the same sort, "these," he said, "do not deserve to be burned like the others, for they neither do nor can do the mischief the books of chivalry have done, being books of entertainment that can hurt no one."

"Ah, senor!" said the niece, "your worship had better order these to be burned as well as the others; for it would be no wonder if, after being cured of his chivalry disorder, my uncle, by reading these, took a fancy to turn shepherd and range the woods and fields singing and piping; or, what would be still worse, to turn poet, which they say is an incurable and infectious malady."

"The damsel is right," said the curate, "and it will be well to put this stumbling-block and temptation out of our friend's way. To begin, then, with the 'Diana' of Montemayor. I am of opinion it should not be burned, but that it should be cleared of all that about the sage Felicia and the magic water, and of almost all the longer pieces of verse: let it keep, and welcome, its prose and the honour of being the first of books of the kind."

"This that comes next," said the barber, "is the 'Diana,' entitled the 'Second Part, by the Salamancan,' and this other has the same title, and its author is Gil Polo."

"As for that of the Salamancan," replied the curate, "let it go to swell the number of the condemned in the yard, and let Gil Polo's be preserved as if it came from Apollo himself: but get on, gossip, and make haste, for it is growing late."

"This book," said the barber, opening another, "is the ten books of the

'Fortune of Love,' written by Antonio de Lofraso, a Sardinian poet."

"By the orders I have received," said the curate, "since Apollo has been Apollo, and the Muses have been Muses, and poets have been poets, so droll and absurd a book as this has never been written, and in its way it is the best and the most singular of all of this species that have as yet appeared, and he who has not read it may be sure he has never read what is delightful. Give it here, gossip, for I make more account of having found it than if they had given me a cassock of Florence stuff."

He put it aside with extreme satisfaction, and the barber went on, "These that come next are 'The Shepherd of Iberia,' 'Nymphs of Henares,' and 'The Enlightenment of Jealousy.'"

"Then all we have to do," said the curate, "is to hand them over to the secular arm of the housekeeper, and ask me not why, or we shall never have done."

"This next is the 'Pastor de Filida.'"

"No Pastor that," said the curate, "but a highly polished courtier; let it be preserved as a precious jewel."

"This large one here," said the barber, "is called 'The Treasury of various Poems.'"

"If there were not so many of them," said the curate, "they would be more relished: this book must be weeded and cleansed of certain vulgarities which it has with its excellences; let it be preserved because the author is a friend of mine, and out of respect for other more heroic and loftier works that he has written."

"This," continued the barber, "is the 'Cancionero' of Lopez de

Maldonado."

"The author of that book, too," said the curate, "is a great friend of mine, and his verses from his own mouth are the admiration of all who hear them, for such is the sweetness of his voice that he enchants when he chants them: it gives rather too much of its eclogues, but what is good was never yet plentiful: let it be kept with those that have been set apart. But what book is that next it?"

"The 'Galatea' of Miguel de Cervantes," said the barber.

"That Cervantes has been for many years a great friend of mine, and to my knowledge he has had more experience in reverses than in verses. His book has some good invention in it, it presents us with something but brings nothing to a conclusion: we must wait for the Second Part it promises: perhaps with amendment it may succeed in winning the full measure of grace that is now denied it; and in the mean time do you, senor gossip, keep it shut up in your own quarters."

"Very good," said the barber; "and here come three together, the

'Araucana' of Don Alonso de Ercilla, the 'Austriada' of Juan Rufo,

Justice of Cordova, and the 'Montserrate' of Christobal de Virues, the

Valencian poet."

"These three books," said the curate, "are the best that have been written in Castilian in heroic verse, and they may compare with the most famous of Italy; let them be preserved as the richest treasures of poetry that Spain possesses."

The curate was tired and would not look into any more books, and so he decided that, "contents uncertified," all the rest should be burned; but just then the barber held open one, called "The Tears of Angelica."

"I should have shed tears myself," said the curate when he heard the title, "had I ordered that book to be burned, for its author was one of the famous poets of the world, not to say of Spain, and was very happy in the translation of some of Ovid's fables."

CHAPTER VII.

OF THE SECOND SALLY OF OUR WORTHY KNIGHT DON QUIXOTE OF LA MANCHA

At this instant Don Quixote began shouting out, "Here, here, valiant knights! here is need for you to put forth the might of your strong arms, for they of the Court are gaining the mastery in the tourney!" Called away by this noise and outcry, they proceeded no farther with the scrutiny of the remaining books, and so it is thought that "The Carolea," "The Lion of Spain," and "The Deeds of the Emperor," written by Don Luis de Avila, went to the fire unseen and unheard; for no doubt they were among those that remained, and perhaps if the curate had seen them they would not have undergone so severe a sentence.

When they reached Don Quixote he was already out of bed, and was still shouting and raving, and slashing and cutting all round, as wide awake as if he had never slept.

They closed with him and by force got him back to bed, and when he had become a little calm, addressing the curate, he said to him, "Of a truth, Senor Archbishop Turpin, it is a great disgrace for us who call ourselves the Twelve Peers, so carelessly to allow the knights of the Court to gain the victory in this tourney, we the adventurers having carried off the honour on the three former days."

"Hush, gossip," said the curate; "please God, the luck may turn, and what is lost to-day may be won to-morrow; for the present let your worship have a care of your health, for it seems to me that you are over-fatigued, if not badly wounded."

"Wounded no," said Don Quixote, "but bruised and battered no doubt, for that bastard Don Roland has cudgelled me with the trunk of an oak tree, and all for envy, because he sees that I alone rival him in his achievements. But I should not call myself Reinaldos of Montalvan did he not pay me for it in spite of all his enchantments as soon as I rise from this bed. For the present let them bring me something to eat, for that, I feel, is what will be more to my purpose, and leave it to me to avenge myself."

They did as he wished; they gave him something to eat, and once more he fell asleep, leaving them marvelling at his madness.

That night the housekeeper burned to ashes all the books that were in the yard and in the whole house; and some must have been consumed that deserved preservation in everlasting archives, but their fate and the laziness of the examiner did not permit it, and so in them was verified the proverb that the innocent suffer for the guilty.

One of the remedies which the curate and the barber immediately applied to their friend's disorder was to wall up and plaster the room where the books were, so that when he got up he should not find them (possibly the cause being removed the effect might cease), and they might say that a magician had carried them off, room and all; and this was done with all despatch. Two days later Don Quixote got up, and the first thing he did was to go and look at his books, and not finding the room where he had left it, he wandered from side to side looking for it. He came to the place where the door used to be, and tried it with his hands, and turned and twisted his eyes in every direction without saying a word; but after a good while he asked his housekeeper whereabouts was the room that held his books.

The housekeeper, who had been already well instructed in what she was to answer, said, "What room or what nothing is it that your worship is looking for? There are neither room nor books in this house now, for the devil himself has carried all away."

"It was not the devil," said the niece, "but a magician who came on a cloud one night after the day your worship left this, and dismounting from a serpent that he rode he entered the room, and what he did there I know not, but after a little while he made off, flying through the roof, and left the house full of smoke; and when we went to see what he had done we saw neither book nor room: but we remember very well, the housekeeper and I, that on leaving, the old villain said in a loud voice that, for a private grudge he owed the owner of the books and the room, he had done mischief in that house that would be discovered by-and-by: he said too that his name was the Sage Munaton."

"He must have said Friston," said Don Quixote.

"I don't know whether he called himself Friston or Friton," said the housekeeper, "I only know that his name ended with 'ton.'"

"So it does," said Don Quixote, "and he is a sage magician, a great enemy of mine, who has a spite against me because he knows by his arts and lore that in process of time I am to engage in single combat with a knight whom he befriends and that I am to conquer, and he will be unable to prevent it; and for this reason he endeavours to do me all the ill turns that he can; but I promise him it will be hard for him to oppose or avoid what is decreed by Heaven."

"Who doubts that?" said the niece; "but, uncle, who mixes you up in these quarrels? Would it not be better to remain at peace in your own house instead of roaming the world looking for better bread than ever came of wheat, never reflecting that many go for wool and come back shorn?"

"Oh, niece of mine," replied Don Quixote, "how much astray art thou in thy reckoning: ere they shear me I shall have plucked away and stripped off the beards of all who dare to touch only the tip of a hair of mine."

The two were unwilling to make any further answer, as they saw that his anger was kindling.

In short, then, he remained at home fifteen days very quietly without showing any signs of a desire to take up with his former delusions, and during this time he held lively discussions with his two gossips, the curate and the barber, on the point he maintained, that knights-errant were what the world stood most in need of, and that in him was to be accomplished the revival of knight-errantry. The curate sometimes contradicted him, sometimes agreed with him, for if he had not observed this precaution he would have been unable to bring him to reason.

Meanwhile Don Quixote worked upon a farm labourer, a neighbour of his, an honest man (if indeed that title can be given to him who is poor), but with very little wit in his pate. In a word, he so talked him over, and with such persuasions and promises, that the poor clown made up his mind to sally forth with him and serve him as esquire. Don Quixote, among other things, told him he ought to be ready to go with him gladly, because any moment an adventure might occur that might win an island in the twinkling of an eye and leave him governor of it. On these and the like promises Sancho Panza (for so the labourer was called) left wife and children, and engaged himself as esquire to his neighbour.

Don Quixote next set about getting some money; and selling one thing and pawning another, and making a bad bargain in every case, he got together a fair sum. He provided himself with a buckler, which he begged as a loan from a friend, and, restoring his battered helmet as best he could, he warned his squire Sancho of the day and hour he meant to set out, that he might provide himself with what he thought most needful. Above all, he charged him to take alforjas with him. The other said he would, and that he meant to take also a very good ass he had, as he was not much given to going on foot. About the ass, Don Quixote hesitated a little, trying whether he could call to mind any knight-errant taking with him an esquire mounted on ass-back, but no instance occurred to his memory. For all that, however, he determined to take him, intending to furnish him with a more honourable mount when a chance of it presented itself, by appropriating the horse of the first discourteous knight he encountered. Himself he provided with shirts and such other things as he could, according to the advice the host had given him; all which being done, without taking leave, Sancho Panza of his wife and children, or Don Quixote of his housekeeper and niece, they sallied forth unseen by anybody from the village one night, and made such good way in the course of it that by daylight they held themselves safe from discovery, even should search be made for them.

Sancho rode on his ass like a patriarch, with his alforjas and bota, and longing to see himself soon governor of the island his master had promised him. Don Quixote decided upon taking the same route and road he had taken on his first journey, that over the Campo de Montiel, which he travelled with less discomfort than on the last occasion, for, as it was early morning and the rays of the sun fell on them obliquely, the heat did not distress them.

And now said Sancho Panza to his master, "Your worship will take care, Senor Knight-errant, not to forget about the island you have promised me, for be it ever so big I'll be equal to governing it."

To which Don Quixote replied, "Thou must know, friend Sancho Panza, that it was a practice very much in vogue with the knights-errant of old to make their squires governors of the islands or kingdoms they won, and I am determined that there shall be no failure on my part in so liberal a custom; on the contrary, I mean to improve upon it, for they sometimes, and perhaps most frequently, waited until their squires were old, and then when they had had enough of service and hard days and worse nights, they gave them some title or other, of count, or at the most marquis, of some valley or province more or less; but if thou livest and I live, it may well be that before six days are over, I may have won some kingdom that has others dependent upon it, which will be just the thing to enable thee to be crowned king of one of them. Nor needst thou count this wonderful, for things and chances fall to the lot of such knights in ways so unexampled and unexpected that I might easily give thee even more than I promise thee."

"In that case," said Sancho Panza, "if I should become a king by one of those miracles your worship speaks of, even Juana Gutierrez, my old woman, would come to be queen and my children infantes."

"Well, who doubts it?" said Don Quixote.

"I doubt it," replied Sancho Panza, "because for my part I am persuaded that though God should shower down kingdoms upon earth, not one of them would fit the head of Mari Gutierrez. Let me tell you, senor, she is not worth two maravedis for a queen; countess will fit her better, and that only with God's help."

"Leave it to God, Sancho," returned Don Quixote, "for he will give her what suits her best; but do not undervalue thyself so much as to come to be content with anything less than being governor of a province."

"I will not, senor," answered Sancho, "specially as I have a man of such quality for a master in your worship, who will know how to give me all that will be suitable for me and that I can bear."

CHAPTER VIII.

OF THE GOOD FORTUNE WHICH THE VALIANT DON QUIXOTE HAD IN THE TERRIBLE AND UNDREAMT-OF ADVENTURE OF THE WINDMILLS, WITH OTHER OCCURRENCES WORTHY TO BE FITLY RECORDED

At this point they came in sight of thirty forty windmills that there are on plain, and as soon as Don Quixote saw them he said to his squire, "Fortune is arranging matters for us better than we could have shaped our desires ourselves, for look there, friend Sancho Panza, where thirty or more monstrous giants present themselves, all of whom I mean to engage in battle and slay, and with whose spoils we shall begin to make our fortunes; for this is righteous warfare, and it is God's good service to sweep so evil a breed from off the face of the earth."

"What giants?" said Sancho Panza.

"Those thou seest there," answered his master, "with the long arms, and some have them nearly two leagues long."

"Look, your worship," said Sancho; "what we see there are not giants but windmills, and what seem to be their arms are the sails that turned by the wind make the millstone go."

"It is easy to see," replied Don Quixote, "that thou art not used to this business of adventures; those are giants; and if thou art afraid, away with thee out of this and betake thyself to prayer while I engage them in fierce and unequal combat."

So saying, he gave the spur to his steed Rocinante, heedless of the cries his squire Sancho sent after him, warning him that most certainly they were windmills and not giants he was going to attack. He, however, was so positive they were giants that he neither heard the cries of Sancho, nor perceived, near as he was, what they were, but made at them shouting, "Fly not, cowards and vile beings, for a single knight attacks you."

A slight breeze at this moment sprang up, and the great sails began to move, seeing which Don Quixote exclaimed, "Though ye flourish more arms than the giant Briareus, ye have to reckon with me."

So saying, and commending himself with all his heart to his lady Dulcinea, imploring her to support him in such a peril, with lance in rest and covered by his buckler, he charged at Rocinante's fullest gallop and fell upon the first mill that stood in front of him; but as he drove his lance-point into the sail the wind whirled it round with such force that it shivered the lance to pieces, sweeping with it horse and rider, who went rolling over on the plain, in a sorry condition. Sancho hastened to his assistance as fast as his ass could go, and when he came up found him unable to move, with such a shock had Rocinante fallen with him.

"God bless me!" said Sancho, "did I not tell your worship to mind what you were about, for they were only windmills? and no one could have made any mistake about it but one who had something of the same kind in his head."

"Hush, friend Sancho," replied Don Quixote, "the fortunes of war more than any other are liable to frequent fluctuations; and moreover I think, and it is the truth, that that same sage Friston who carried off my study and books, has turned these giants into mills in order to rob me of the glory of vanquishing them, such is the enmity he bears me; but in the end his wicked arts will avail but little against my good sword."

"God order it as he may," said Sancho Panza, and helping him to rise got him up again on Rocinante, whose shoulder was half out; and then, discussing the late adventure, they followed the road to Puerto Lapice, for there, said Don Quixote, they could not fail to find adventures in abundance and variety, as it was a great thoroughfare. For all that, he was much grieved at the loss of his lance, and saying so to his squire, he added, "I remember having read how a Spanish knight, Diego Perez de Vargas by name, having broken his sword in battle, tore from an oak a ponderous bough or branch, and with it did such things that day, and pounded so many Moors, that he got the surname of Machuca, and he and his descendants from that day forth were called Vargas y Machuca. I mention this because from the first oak I see I mean to rend such another branch, large and stout like that, with which I am determined and resolved to do such deeds that thou mayest deem thyself very fortunate in being found worthy to come and see them, and be an eyewitness of things that will with difficulty be believed."

"Be that as God will," said Sancho, "I believe it all as your worship says it; but straighten yourself a little, for you seem all on one side, may be from the shaking of the fall."

"That is the truth," said Don Quixote, "and if I make no complaint of the pain it is because knights-errant are not permitted to complain of any wound, even though their bowels be coming out through it."

"If so," said Sancho, "I have nothing to say; but God knows I would rather your worship complained when anything ailed you. For my part, I confess I must complain however small the ache may be; unless this rule about not complaining extends to the squires of knights-errant also."

Don Quixote could not help laughing at his squire's simplicity, and he assured him he might complain whenever and however he chose, just as he liked, for, so far, he had never read of anything to the contrary in the order of knighthood.

Sancho bade him remember it was dinner-time, to which his master answered that he wanted nothing himself just then, but that he might eat when he had a mind. With this permission Sancho settled himself as comfortably as he could on his beast, and taking out of the alforjas what he had stowed away in them, he jogged along behind his master munching deliberately, and from time to time taking a pull at the bota with a relish that the thirstiest tapster in Malaga might have envied; and while he went on in this way, gulping down draught after draught, he never gave a thought to any of the promises his master had made him, nor did he rate it as hardship but rather as recreation going in quest of adventures, however dangerous they might be. Finally they passed the night among some trees, from one of which Don Quixote plucked a dry branch to serve him after a fashion as a lance, and fixed on it the head he had removed from the broken one. All that night Don Quixote lay awake thinking of his lady Dulcinea, in order to conform to what he had read in his books, how many a night in the forests and deserts knights used to lie sleepless supported by the memory of their mistresses. Not so did Sancho Panza spend it, for having his stomach full of something stronger than chicory water he made but one sleep of it, and, if his master had not called him, neither the rays of the sun beating on his face nor all the cheery notes of the birds welcoming the approach of day would have had power to waken him. On getting up he tried the bota and found it somewhat less full than the night before, which grieved his heart because they did not seem to be on the way to remedy the deficiency readily. Don Quixote did not care to break his fast, for, as has been already said, he confined himself to savoury recollections for nourishment.

They returned to the road they had set out with, leading to Puerto Lapice, and at three in the afternoon they came in sight of it. "Here, brother Sancho Panza," said Don Quixote when he saw it, "we may plunge our hands up to the elbows in what they call adventures; but observe, even shouldst thou see me in the greatest danger in the world, thou must not put a hand to thy sword in my defence, unless indeed thou perceivest that those who assail me are rabble or base folk; for in that case thou mayest very properly aid me; but if they be knights it is on no account permitted or allowed thee by the laws of knighthood to help me until thou hast been dubbed a knight."

"Most certainly, senor," replied Sancho, "your worship shall be fully obeyed in this matter; all the more as of myself I am peaceful and no friend to mixing in strife and quarrels: it is true that as regards the defence of my own person I shall not give much heed to those laws, for laws human and divine allow each one to defend himself against any assailant whatever."

"That I grant," said Don Quixote, "but in this matter of aiding me against knights thou must put a restraint upon thy natural impetuosity."

"I will do so, I promise you," answered Sancho, "and will keep this precept as carefully as Sunday."

While they were thus talking there appeared on the road two friars of the order of St. Benedict, mounted on two dromedaries, for not less tall were the two mules they rode on. They wore travelling spectacles and carried sunshades; and behind them came a coach attended by four or five persons on horseback and two muleteers on foot. In the coach there was, as afterwards appeared, a Biscay lady on her way to Seville, where her husband was about to take passage for the Indies with an appointment of high honour. The friars, though going the same road, were not in her company; but the moment Don Quixote perceived them he said to his squire, "Either I am mistaken, or this is going to be the most famous adventure that has ever been seen, for those black bodies we see there must be, and doubtless are, magicians who are carrying off some stolen princess in that coach, and with all my might I must undo this wrong."

"This will be worse than the windmills," said Sancho. "Look, senor; those are friars of St. Benedict, and the coach plainly belongs to some travellers: I tell you to mind well what you are about and don't let the devil mislead you."

"I have told thee already, Sancho," replied Don Quixote, "that on the subject of adventures thou knowest little. What I say is the truth, as thou shalt see presently."

So saying, he advanced and posted himself in the middle of the road along which the friars were coming, and as soon as he thought they had come near enough to hear what he said, he cried aloud, "Devilish and unnatural beings, release instantly the highborn princesses whom you are carrying off by force in this coach, else prepare to meet a speedy death as the just punishment of your evil deeds."

The friars drew rein and stood wondering at the appearance of Don Quixote as well as at his words, to which they replied, "Senor Caballero, we are not devilish or unnatural, but two brothers of St. Benedict following our road, nor do we know whether or not there are any captive princesses coming in this coach."

"No soft words with me, for I know you, lying rabble," said Don Quixote, and without waiting for a reply he spurred Rocinante and with levelled lance charged the first friar with such fury and determination, that, if the friar had not flung himself off the mule, he would have brought him to the ground against his will, and sore wounded, if not killed outright. The second brother, seeing how his comrade was treated, drove his heels into his castle of a mule and made off across the country faster than the wind.

Sancho Panza, when he saw the friar on the ground, dismounting briskly from his ass, rushed towards him and began to strip off his gown. At that instant the friars muleteers came up and asked what he was stripping him for. Sancho answered them that this fell to him lawfully as spoil of the battle which his lord Don Quixote had won. The muleteers, who had no idea of a joke and did not understand all this about battles and spoils, seeing that Don Quixote was some distance off talking to the travellers in the coach, fell upon Sancho, knocked him down, and leaving hardly a hair in his beard, belaboured him with kicks and left him stretched breathless and senseless on the ground; and without any more delay helped the friar to mount, who, trembling, terrified, and pale, as soon as he found himself in the saddle, spurred after his companion, who was standing at a distance looking on, watching the result of the onslaught; then, not caring to wait for the end of the affair just begun, they pursued their journey making more crosses than if they had the devil after them.

Don Quixote was, as has been said, speaking to the lady in the coach: "Your beauty, lady mine," said he, "may now dispose of your person as may be most in accordance with your pleasure, for the pride of your ravishers lies prostrate on the ground through this strong arm of mine; and lest you should be pining to know the name of your deliverer, know that I am called Don Quixote of La Mancha, knight-errant and adventurer, and captive to the peerless and beautiful lady Dulcinea del Toboso: and in return for the service you have received of me I ask no more than that you should return to El Toboso, and on my behalf present yourself before that lady and tell her what I have done to set you free."

One of the squires in attendance upon the coach, a Biscayan, was listening to all Don Quixote was saying, and, perceiving that he would not allow the coach to go on, but was saying it must return at once to El Toboso, he made at him, and seizing his lance addressed him in bad Castilian and worse Biscayan after his fashion, "Begone, caballero, and ill go with thee; by the God that made me, unless thou quittest coach, slayest thee as art here a Biscayan."

Don Quixote understood him quite well, and answered him very quietly, "If thou wert a knight, as thou art none, I should have already chastised thy folly and rashness, miserable creature." To which the Biscayan returned, "I no gentleman!—I swear to God thou liest as I am Christian: if thou droppest lance and drawest sword, soon shalt thou see thou art carrying water to the cat: Biscayan on land, hidalgo at sea, hidalgo at the devil, and look, if thou sayest otherwise thou liest."

"'"You will see presently," said Agrajes,'" replied Don Quixote; and throwing his lance on the ground he drew his sword, braced his buckler on his arm, and attacked the Biscayan, bent upon taking his life.

The Biscayan, when he saw him coming on, though he wished to dismount from his mule, in which, being one of those sorry ones let out for hire, he had no confidence, had no choice but to draw his sword; it was lucky for him, however, that he was near the coach, from which he was able to snatch a cushion that served him for a shield; and they went at one another as if they had been two mortal enemies. The others strove to make peace between them, but could not, for the Biscayan declared in his disjointed phrase that if they did not let him finish his battle he would kill his mistress and everyone that strove to prevent him. The lady in the coach, amazed and terrified at what she saw, ordered the coachman to draw aside a little, and set herself to watch this severe struggle, in the course of which the Biscayan smote Don Quixote a mighty stroke on the shoulder over the top of his buckler, which, given to one without armour, would have cleft him to the waist. Don Quixote, feeling the weight of this prodigious blow, cried aloud, saying, "O lady of my soul, Dulcinea, flower of beauty, come to the aid of this your knight, who, in fulfilling his obligations to your beauty, finds himself in this extreme peril." To say this, to lift his sword, to shelter himself well behind his buckler, and to assail the Biscayan was the work of an instant, determined as he was to venture all upon a single blow. The Biscayan, seeing him come on in this way, was convinced of his courage by his spirited bearing, and resolved to follow his example, so he waited for him keeping well under cover of his cushion, being unable to execute any sort of manoeuvre with his mule, which, dead tired and never meant for this kind of game, could not stir a step.

On, then, as aforesaid, came Don Quixote against the wary Biscayan, with uplifted sword and a firm intention of splitting him in half, while on his side the Biscayan waited for him sword in hand, and under the protection of his cushion; and all present stood trembling, waiting in suspense the result of blows such as threatened to fall, and the lady in the coach and the rest of her following were making a thousand vows and offerings to all the images and shrines of Spain, that God might deliver her squire and all of them from this great peril in which they found themselves. But it spoils all, that at this point and crisis the author of the history leaves this battle impending, giving as excuse that he could find nothing more written about these achievements of Don Quixote than what has been already set forth. It is true the second author of this work was unwilling to believe that a history so curious could have been allowed to fall under the sentence of oblivion, or that the wits of La Mancha could have been so undiscerning as not to preserve in their archives or registries some documents referring to this famous knight; and this being his persuasion, he did not despair of finding the conclusion of this pleasant history, which, heaven favouring him, he did find in a way that shall be related in the Second Part.

CHAPTER IX.

IN WHICH IS CONCLUDED AND FINISHED THE TERRIFIC BATTLE BETWEEN THE GALLANT BISCAYAN AND THE VALIANT MANCHEGAN

In the First Part of this history we left the valiant Biscayan and the renowned Don Quixote with drawn swords uplifted, ready to deliver two such furious slashing blows that if they had fallen full and fair they would at least have split and cleft them asunder from top to toe and laid them open like a pomegranate; and at this so critical point the delightful history came to a stop and stood cut short without any intimation from the author where what was missing was to be found.

This distressed me greatly, because the pleasure derived from having read such a small portion turned to vexation at the thought of the poor chance that presented itself of finding the large part that, so it seemed to me, was missing of such an interesting tale. It appeared to me to be a thing impossible and contrary to all precedent that so good a knight should have been without some sage to undertake the task of writing his marvellous achievements; a thing that was never wanting to any of those knights-errant who, they say, went after adventures; for every one of them had one or two sages as if made on purpose, who not only recorded their deeds but described their most trifling thoughts and follies, however secret they might be; and such a good knight could not have been so unfortunate as not to have what Platir and others like him had in abundance. And so I could not bring myself to believe that such a gallant tale had been left maimed and mutilated, and I laid the blame on Time, the devourer and destroyer of all things, that had either concealed or consumed it.

On the other hand, it struck me that, inasmuch as among his books there had been found such modern ones as "The Enlightenment of Jealousy" and the "Nymphs and Shepherds of Henares," his story must likewise be modern, and that though it might not be written, it might exist in the memory of the people of his village and of those in the neighbourhood. This reflection kept me perplexed and longing to know really and truly the whole life and wondrous deeds of our famous Spaniard, Don Quixote of La Mancha, light and mirror of Manchegan chivalry, and the first that in our age and in these so evil days devoted himself to the labour and exercise of the arms of knight-errantry, righting wrongs, succouring widows, and protecting damsels of that sort that used to ride about, whip in hand, on their palfreys, with all their virginity about them, from mountain to mountain and valley to valley—for, if it were not for some ruffian, or boor with a hood and hatchet, or monstrous giant, that forced them, there were in days of yore damsels that at the end of eighty years, in all which time they had never slept a day under a roof, went to their graves as much maids as the mothers that bore them. I say, then, that in these and other respects our gallant Don Quixote is worthy of everlasting and notable praise, nor should it be withheld even from me for the labour and pains spent in searching for the conclusion of this delightful history; though I know well that if Heaven, chance and good fortune had not helped me, the world would have remained deprived of an entertainment and pleasure that for a couple of hours or so may well occupy him who shall read it attentively. The discovery of it occurred in this way.

One day, as I was in the Alcana of Toledo, a boy came up to sell some pamphlets and old papers to a silk mercer, and, as I am fond of reading even the very scraps of paper in the streets, led by this natural bent of mine I took up one of the pamphlets the boy had for sale, and saw that it was in characters which I recognised as Arabic, and as I was unable to read them though I could recognise them, I looked about to see if there were any Spanish-speaking Morisco at hand to read them for me; nor was there any great difficulty in finding such an interpreter, for even had I sought one for an older and better language I should have found him. In short, chance provided me with one, who when I told him what I wanted and put the book into his hands, opened it in the middle and after reading a little in it began to laugh. I asked him what he was laughing at, and he replied that it was at something the book had written in the margin by way of a note. I bade him tell it to me; and he still laughing said, "In the margin, as I told you, this is written: 'This Dulcinea del Toboso so often mentioned in this history, had, they say, the best hand of any woman in all La Mancha for salting pigs.'"

When I heard Dulcinea del Toboso named, I was struck with surprise and amazement, for it occurred to me at once that these pamphlets contained the history of Don Quixote. With this idea I pressed him to read the beginning, and doing so, turning the Arabic offhand into Castilian, he told me it meant, "History of Don Quixote of La Mancha, written by Cide Hamete Benengeli, an Arab historian." It required great caution to hide the joy I felt when the title of the book reached my ears, and snatching it from the silk mercer, I bought all the papers and pamphlets from the boy for half a real; and if he had had his wits about him and had known how eager I was for them, he might have safely calculated on making more than six reals by the bargain. I withdrew at once with the Morisco into the cloister of the cathedral, and begged him to turn all these pamphlets that related to Don Quixote into the Castilian tongue, without omitting or adding anything to them, offering him whatever payment he pleased. He was satisfied with two arrobas of raisins and two bushels of wheat, and promised to translate them faithfully and with all despatch; but to make the matter easier, and not to let such a precious find out of my hands, I took him to my house, where in little more than a month and a half he translated the whole just as it is set down here.

In the first pamphlet the battle between Don Quixote and the Biscayan was drawn to the very life, they planted in the same attitude as the history describes, their swords raised, and the one protected by his buckler, the other by his cushion, and the Biscayan's mule so true to nature that it could be seen to be a hired one a bowshot off. The Biscayan had an inscription under his feet which said, "Don Sancho de Azpeitia," which no doubt must have been his name; and at the feet of Rocinante was another that said, "Don Quixote." Rocinante was marvellously portrayed, so long and thin, so lank and lean, with so much backbone and so far gone in consumption, that he showed plainly with what judgment and propriety the name of Rocinante had been bestowed upon him. Near him was Sancho Panza holding the halter of his ass, at whose feet was another label that said, "Sancho Zancas," and according to the picture, he must have had a big belly, a short body, and long shanks, for which reason, no doubt, the names of Panza and Zancas were given him, for by these two surnames the history several times calls him. Some other trifling particulars might be mentioned, but they are all of slight importance and have nothing to do with the true relation of the history; and no history can be bad so long as it is true.

If against the present one any objection be raised on the score of its truth, it can only be that its author was an Arab, as lying is a very common propensity with those of that nation; though, as they are such enemies of ours, it is conceivable that there were omissions rather than additions made in the course of it. And this is my own opinion; for, where he could and should give freedom to his pen in praise of so worthy a knight, he seems to me deliberately to pass it over in silence; which is ill done and worse contrived, for it is the business and duty of historians to be exact, truthful, and wholly free from passion, and neither interest nor fear, hatred nor love, should make them swerve from the path of truth, whose mother is history, rival of time, storehouse of deeds, witness for the past, example and counsel for the present, and warning for the future. In this I know will be found all that can be desired in the pleasantest, and if it be wanting in any good quality, I maintain it is the fault of its hound of an author and not the fault of the subject. To be brief, its Second Part, according to the translation, began in this way:

With trenchant swords upraised and poised on high, it seemed as though the two valiant and wrathful combatants stood threatening heaven, and earth, and hell, with such resolution and determination did they bear themselves. The fiery Biscayan was the first to strike a blow, which was delivered with such force and fury that had not the sword turned in its course, that single stroke would have sufficed to put an end to the bitter struggle and to all the adventures of our knight; but that good fortune which reserved him for greater things, turned aside the sword of his adversary, so that although it smote him upon the left shoulder, it did him no more harm than to strip all that side of its armour, carrying away a great part of his helmet with half of his ear, all which with fearful ruin fell to the ground, leaving him in a sorry plight.

Good God! Who is there that could properly describe the rage that filled the heart of our Manchegan when he saw himself dealt with in this fashion? All that can be said is, it was such that he again raised himself in his stirrups, and, grasping his sword more firmly with both hands, he came down on the Biscayan with such fury, smiting him full over the cushion and over the head, that—even so good a shield proving useless—as if a mountain had fallen on him, he began to bleed from nose, mouth, and ears, reeling as if about to fall backwards from his mule, as no doubt he would have done had he not flung his arms about its neck; at the same time, however, he slipped his feet out of the stirrups and then unclasped his arms, and the mule, taking fright at the terrible blow, made off across the plain, and with a few plunges flung its master to the ground. Don Quixote stood looking on very calmly, and, when he saw him fall, leaped from his horse and with great briskness ran to him, and, presenting the point of his sword to his eyes, bade him surrender, or he would cut his head off. The Biscayan was so bewildered that he was unable to answer a word, and it would have gone hard with him, so blind was Don Quixote, had not the ladies in the coach, who had hitherto been watching the combat in great terror, hastened to where he stood and implored him with earnest entreaties to grant them the great grace and favour of sparing their squire's life; to which Don Quixote replied with much gravity and dignity, "In truth, fair ladies, I am well content to do what ye ask of me; but it must be on one condition and understanding, which is that this knight promise me to go to the village of El Toboso, and on my behalf present himself before the peerless lady Dulcinea, that she deal with him as shall be most pleasing to her."

The terrified and disconsolate ladies, without discussing Don Quixote's demand or asking who Dulcinea might be, promised that their squire should do all that had been commanded.

"Then, on the faith of that promise," said Don Quixote, "I shall do him no further harm, though he well deserves it of me."

CHAPTER X.

OF THE PLEASANT DISCOURSE THAT PASSED BETWEEN DON QUIXOTE AND HIS SQUIRE SANCHO PANZA

Now by this time Sancho had risen, rather the worse for the handling of the friars' muleteers, and stood watching the battle of his master, Don Quixote, and praying to God in his heart that it might be his will to grant him the victory, and that he might thereby win some island to make him governor of, as he had promised. Seeing, therefore, that the struggle was now over, and that his master was returning to mount Rocinante, he approached to hold the stirrup for him, and, before he could mount, he went on his knees before him, and taking his hand, kissed it saying, "May it please your worship, Senor Don Quixote, to give me the government of that island which has been won in this hard fight, for be it ever so big I feel myself in sufficient force to be able to govern it as much and as well as anyone in the world who has ever governed islands."

To which Don Quixote replied, "Thou must take notice, brother Sancho, that this adventure and those like it are not adventures of islands, but of cross-roads, in which nothing is got except a broken head or an ear the less: have patience, for adventures will present themselves from which I may make you, not only a governor, but something more."

Sancho gave him many thanks, and again kissing his hand and the skirt of his hauberk, helped him to mount Rocinante, and mounting his ass himself, proceeded to follow his master, who at a brisk pace, without taking leave, or saying anything further to the ladies belonging to the coach, turned into a wood that was hard by. Sancho followed him at his ass's best trot, but Rocinante stepped out so that, seeing himself left behind, he was forced to call to his master to wait for him. Don Quixote did so, reining in Rocinante until his weary squire came up, who on reaching him said, "It seems to me, senor, it would be prudent in us to go and take refuge in some church, for, seeing how mauled he with whom you fought has been left, it will be no wonder if they give information of the affair to the Holy Brotherhood and arrest us, and, faith, if they do, before we come out of gaol we shall have to sweat for it."

"Peace," said Don Quixote; "where hast thou ever seen or heard that a knight-errant has been arraigned before a court of justice, however many homicides he may have committed?"

"I know nothing about omecils," answered Sancho, "nor in my life have had anything to do with one; I only know that the Holy Brotherhood looks after those who fight in the fields, and in that other matter I do not meddle."

"Then thou needst have no uneasiness, my friend," said Don Quixote, "for I will deliver thee out of the hands of the Chaldeans, much more out of those of the Brotherhood. But tell me, as thou livest, hast thou seen a more valiant knight than I in all the known world; hast thou read in history of any who has or had higher mettle in attack, more spirit in maintaining it, more dexterity in wounding or skill in overthrowing?"

"The truth is," answered Sancho, "that I have never read any history, for I can neither read nor write, but what I will venture to bet is that a more daring master than your worship I have never served in all the days of my life, and God grant that this daring be not paid for where I have said; what I beg of your worship is to dress your wound, for a great deal of blood flows from that ear, and I have here some lint and a little white ointment in the alforjas."

"All that might be well dispensed with," said Don Quixote, "if I had remembered to make a vial of the balsam of Fierabras, for time and medicine are saved by one single drop."

"What vial and what balsam is that?" said Sancho Panza.

"It is a balsam," answered Don Quixote, "the receipt of which I have in my memory, with which one need have no fear of death, or dread dying of any wound; and so when I make it and give it to thee thou hast nothing to do when in some battle thou seest they have cut me in half through the middle of the body—as is wont to happen frequently,—but neatly and with great nicety, ere the blood congeal, to place that portion of the body which shall have fallen to the ground upon the other half which remains in the saddle, taking care to fit it on evenly and exactly. Then thou shalt give me to drink but two drops of the balsam I have mentioned, and thou shalt see me become sounder than an apple."

"If that be so," said Panza, "I renounce henceforth the government of the promised island, and desire nothing more in payment of my many and faithful services than that your worship give me the receipt of this supreme liquor, for I am persuaded it will be worth more than two reals an ounce anywhere, and I want no more to pass the rest of my life in ease and honour; but it remains to be told if it costs much to make it."

"With less than three reals, six quarts of it may be made," said Don

Quixote.

"Sinner that I am!" said Sancho, "then why does your worship put off making it and teaching it to me?"

"Peace, friend," answered Don Quixote; "greater secrets I mean to teach thee and greater favours to bestow upon thee; and for the present let us see to the dressing, for my ear pains me more than I could wish."

Sancho took out some lint and ointment from the alforjas; but when Don Quixote came to see his helmet shattered, he was like to lose his senses, and clapping his hand upon his sword and raising his eyes to heaven, be said, "I swear by the Creator of all things and the four Gospels in their fullest extent, to do as the great Marquis of Mantua did when he swore to avenge the death of his nephew Baldwin (and that was not to eat bread from a table-cloth, nor embrace his wife, and other points which, though I cannot now call them to mind, I here grant as expressed) until I take complete vengeance upon him who has committed such an offence against me."

Hearing this, Sancho said to him, "Your worship should bear in mind, Senor Don Quixote, that if the knight has done what was commanded him in going to present himself before my lady Dulcinea del Toboso, he will have done all that he was bound to do, and does not deserve further punishment unless he commits some new offence."

"Thou hast said well and hit the point," answered Don Quixote; and so I recall the oath in so far as relates to taking fresh vengeance on him, but I make and confirm it anew to lead the life I have said until such time as I take by force from some knight another helmet such as this and as good; and think not, Sancho, that I am raising smoke with straw in doing so, for I have one to imitate in the matter, since the very same thing to a hair happened in the case of Mambrino's helmet, which cost Sacripante so dear."

"Senor," replied Sancho, "let your worship send all such oaths to the devil, for they are very pernicious to salvation and prejudicial to the conscience; just tell me now, if for several days to come we fall in with no man armed with a helmet, what are we to do? Is the oath to be observed in spite of all the inconvenience and discomfort it will be to sleep in your clothes, and not to sleep in a house, and a thousand other mortifications contained in the oath of that old fool the Marquis of Mantua, which your worship is now wanting to revive? Let your worship observe that there are no men in armour travelling on any of these roads, nothing but carriers and carters, who not only do not wear helmets, but perhaps never heard tell of them all their lives."

"Thou art wrong there," said Don Quixote, "for we shall not have been above two hours among these cross-roads before we see more men in armour than came to Albraca to win the fair Angelica."

"Enough," said Sancho; "so be it then, and God grant us success, and that the time for winning that island which is costing me so dear may soon come, and then let me die."

"I have already told thee, Sancho," said Don Quixote, "not to give thyself any uneasiness on that score; for if an island should fail, there is the kingdom of Denmark, or of Sobradisa, which will fit thee as a ring fits the finger, and all the more that, being on terra firma, thou wilt all the better enjoy thyself. But let us leave that to its own time; see if thou hast anything for us to eat in those alforjas, because we must presently go in quest of some castle where we may lodge to-night and make the balsam I told thee of, for I swear to thee by God, this ear is giving me great pain."

"I have here an onion and a little cheese and a few scraps of bread," said Sancho, "but they are not victuals fit for a valiant knight like your worship."

"How little thou knowest about it," answered Don Quixote; "I would have thee to know, Sancho, that it is the glory of knights-errant to go without eating for a month, and even when they do eat, that it should be of what comes first to hand; and this would have been clear to thee hadst thou read as many histories as I have, for, though they are very many, among them all I have found no mention made of knights-errant eating, unless by accident or at some sumptuous banquets prepared for them, and the rest of the time they passed in dalliance. And though it is plain they could not do without eating and performing all the other natural functions, because, in fact, they were men like ourselves, it is plain too that, wandering as they did the most part of their lives through woods and wilds and without a cook, their most usual fare would be rustic viands such as those thou now offer me; so that, friend Sancho, let not that distress thee which pleases me, and do not seek to make a new world or pervert knight-errantry."

"Pardon me, your worship," said Sancho, "for, as I cannot read or write, as I said just now, I neither know nor comprehend the rules of the profession of chivalry: henceforward I will stock the alforjas with every kind of dry fruit for your worship, as you are a knight; and for myself, as I am not one, I will furnish them with poultry and other things more substantial."

"I do not say, Sancho," replied Don Quixote, "that it is imperative on knights-errant not to eat anything else but the fruits thou speakest of; only that their more usual diet must be those, and certain herbs they found in the fields which they knew and I know too."

"A good thing it is," answered Sancho, "to know those herbs, for to my thinking it will be needful some day to put that knowledge into practice."

And here taking out what he said he had brought, the pair made their repast peaceably and sociably. But anxious to find quarters for the night, they with all despatch made an end of their poor dry fare, mounted at once, and made haste to reach some habitation before night set in; but daylight and the hope of succeeding in their object failed them close by the huts of some goatherds, so they determined to pass the night there, and it was as much to Sancho's discontent not to have reached a house, as it was to his master's satisfaction to sleep under the open heaven, for he fancied that each time this happened to him he performed an act of ownership that helped to prove his chivalry.

CHAPTER XI.

WHAT BEFELL DON QUIXOTE WITH CERTAIN GOATHERDS

He was cordially welcomed by the goatherds, and Sancho, having as best he could put up Rocinante and the ass, drew towards the fragrance that came from some pieces of salted goat simmering in a pot on the fire; and though he would have liked at once to try if they were ready to be transferred from the pot to the stomach, he refrained from doing so as the goatherds removed them from the fire, and laying sheepskins on the ground, quickly spread their rude table, and with signs of hearty good-will invited them both to share what they had. Round the skins six of the men belonging to the fold seated themselves, having first with rough politeness pressed Don Quixote to take a seat upon a trough which they placed for him upside down. Don Quixote seated himself, and Sancho remained standing to serve the cup, which was made of horn. Seeing him standing, his master said to him:

"That thou mayest see, Sancho, the good that knight-errantry contains in itself, and how those who fill any office in it are on the high road to be speedily honoured and esteemed by the world, I desire that thou seat thyself here at my side and in the company of these worthy people, and that thou be one with me who am thy master and natural lord, and that thou eat from my plate and drink from whatever I drink from; for the same may be said of knight-errantry as of love, that it levels all."

"Great thanks," said Sancho, "but I may tell your worship that provided I have enough to eat, I can eat it as well, or better, standing, and by myself, than seated alongside of an emperor. And indeed, if the truth is to be told, what I eat in my corner without form or fuss has much more relish for me, even though it be bread and onions, than the turkeys of those other tables where I am forced to chew slowly, drink little, wipe my mouth every minute, and cannot sneeze or cough if I want or do other things that are the privileges of liberty and solitude. So, senor, as for these honours which your worship would put upon me as a servant and follower of knight-errantry, exchange them for other things which may be of more use and advantage to me; for these, though I fully acknowledge them as received, I renounce from this moment to the end of the world."

"For all that," said Don Quixote, "thou must seat thyself, because him who humbleth himself God exalteth;" and seizing him by the arm he forced him to sit down beside himself.

The goatherds did not understand this jargon about squires and knights-errant, and all they did was to eat in silence and stare at their guests, who with great elegance and appetite were stowing away pieces as big as one's fist. The course of meat finished, they spread upon the sheepskins a great heap of parched acorns, and with them they put down a half cheese harder than if it had been made of mortar. All this while the horn was not idle, for it went round so constantly, now full, now empty, like the bucket of a water-wheel, that it soon drained one of the two wine-skins that were in sight. When Don Quixote had quite appeased his appetite he took up a handful of the acorns, and contemplating them attentively delivered himself somewhat in this fashion:

"Happy the age, happy the time, to which the ancients gave the name of golden, not because in that fortunate age the gold so coveted in this our iron one was gained without toil, but because they that lived in it knew not the two words "mine" and "thine"! In that blessed age all things were in common; to win the daily food no labour was required of any save to stretch forth his hand and gather it from the sturdy oaks that stood generously inviting him with their sweet ripe fruit. The clear streams and running brooks yielded their savoury limpid waters in noble abundance. The busy and sagacious bees fixed their republic in the clefts of the rocks and hollows of the trees, offering without usance the plenteous produce of their fragrant toil to every hand. The mighty cork trees, unenforced save of their own courtesy, shed the broad light bark that served at first to roof the houses supported by rude stakes, a protection against the inclemency of heaven alone. Then all was peace, all friendship, all concord; as yet the dull share of the crooked plough had not dared to rend and pierce the tender bowels of our first mother that without compulsion yielded from every portion of her broad fertile bosom all that could satisfy, sustain, and delight the children that then possessed her. Then was it that the innocent and fair young shepherdess roamed from vale to vale and hill to hill, with flowing locks, and no more garments than were needful modestly to cover what modesty seeks and ever sought to hide. Nor were their ornaments like those in use to-day, set off by Tyrian purple, and silk tortured in endless fashions, but the wreathed leaves of the green dock and ivy, wherewith they went as bravely and becomingly decked as our Court dames with all the rare and far-fetched artifices that idle curiosity has taught them. Then the love-thoughts of the heart clothed themselves simply and naturally as the heart conceived them, nor sought to commend themselves by forced and rambling verbiage. Fraud, deceit, or malice had then not yet mingled with truth and sincerity. Justice held her ground, undisturbed and unassailed by the efforts of favour and of interest, that now so much impair, pervert, and beset her. Arbitrary law had not yet established itself in the mind of the judge, for then there was no cause to judge and no one to be judged. Maidens and modesty, as I have said, wandered at will alone and unattended, without fear of insult from lawlessness or libertine assault, and if they were undone it was of their own will and pleasure. But now in this hateful age of ours not one is safe, not though some new labyrinth like that of Crete conceal and surround her; even there the pestilence of gallantry will make its way to them through chinks or on the air by the zeal of its accursed importunity, and, despite of all seclusion, lead them to ruin. In defence of these, as time advanced and wickedness increased, the order of knights-errant was instituted, to defend maidens, to protect widows and to succour the orphans and the needy. To this order I belong, brother goatherds, to whom I return thanks for the hospitality and kindly welcome ye offer me and my squire; for though by natural law all living are bound to show favour to knights-errant, yet, seeing that without knowing this obligation ye have welcomed and feasted me, it is right that with all the good-will in my power I should thank you for yours."

All this long harangue (which might very well have been spared) our knight delivered because the acorns they gave him reminded him of the golden age; and the whim seized him to address all this unnecessary argument to the goatherds, who listened to him gaping in amazement without saying a word in reply.

Sancho likewise held his peace and ate acorns, and paid repeated visits to the second wine-skin, which they had hung up on a cork tree to keep the wine cool.

Don Quixote was longer in talking than the supper in finishing, at the end of which one of the goatherds said, "That your worship, senor knight-errant, may say with more truth that we show you hospitality with ready good-will, we will give you amusement and pleasure by making one of our comrades sing: he will be here before long, and he is a very intelligent youth and deep in love, and what is more he can read and write and play on the rebeck to perfection."

The goatherd had hardly done speaking, when the notes of the rebeck reached their ears; and shortly after, the player came up, a very good-looking young man of about two-and-twenty. His comrades asked him if he had supped, and on his replying that he had, he who had already made the offer said to him:

"In that case, Antonio, thou mayest as well do us the pleasure of singing a little, that the gentleman, our guest, may see that even in the mountains and woods there are musicians: we have told him of thy accomplishments, and we want thee to show them and prove that we say true; so, as thou livest, pray sit down and sing that ballad about thy love that thy uncle the prebendary made thee, and that was so much liked in the town."

"With all my heart," said the young man, and without waiting for more pressing he seated himself on the trunk of a felled oak, and tuning his rebeck, presently began to sing to these words.

ANTONIO'S BALLAD

Thou dost love me well, Olalla;
  Well I know it, even though
Love's mute tongues, thine eyes, have never
  By their glances told me so.
For I know my love thou knowest,
  Therefore thine to claim I dare:
Once it ceases to be secret,
  Love need never feel despair.
True it is, Olalla, sometimes

Thou hast all too plainly shown

That thy heart is brass in hardness,

  And thy snowy bosom stone.

Yet for all that, in thy coyness,

  And thy fickle fits between,

Hope is there—at least the border

  Of her garment may be seen.

Lures to faith are they, those glimpses,

  And to faith in thee I hold;

Kindness cannot make it stronger,

  Coldness cannot make it cold.

If it be that love is gentle,

  In thy gentleness I see

Something holding out assurance

  To the hope of winning thee.

If it be that in devotion

  Lies a power hearts to move,

That which every day I show thee,

  Helpful to my suit should prove.

Many a time thou must have noticed—

  If to notice thou dost care—

How I go about on Monday

  Dressed in all my Sunday wear.

Love's eyes love to look on brightness;

  Love loves what is gaily drest;

Sunday, Monday, all I care is

  Thou shouldst see me in my best.

No account I make of dances,

  Or of strains that pleased thee so,

Keeping thee awake from midnight
  Till the cocks began to crow;
Or of how I roundly swore it
  That there's none so fair as thou;
True it is, but as I said it,
  By the girls I'm hated now.

For Teresa of the hillside
  At my praise of thee was sore;
Said, "You think you love an angel;
  It's a monkey you adore;

"Caught by all her glittering trinkets,
  And her borrowed braids of hair,
And a host of made-up beauties
  That would Love himself ensnare."

'T was a lie, and so I told her,
  And her cousin at the word
Gave me his defiance for it;
  And what followed thou hast heard.

Mine is no high-flown affection,
  Mine no passion par amours—
As they call it—what I offer
  Is an honest love, and pure.

Cunning cords the holy Church has,
  Cords of softest silk they be;
Put thy neck beneath the yoke, dear;
  Mine will follow, thou wilt see.

Else—and once for all I swear it
  By the saint of most renown—
If I ever quit the mountains,

'T will be in a friar's gown.

Here the goatherd brought his song to an end, and though Don Quixote entreated him to sing more, Sancho had no mind that way, being more inclined for sleep than for listening to songs; so said he to his master, "Your worship will do well to settle at once where you mean to pass the night, for the labour these good men are at all day does not allow them to spend the night in singing."

"I understand thee, Sancho," replied Don Quixote; "I perceive clearly that those visits to the wine-skin demand compensation in sleep rather than in music."

"It's sweet to us all, blessed be God," said Sancho.

"I do not deny it," replied Don Quixote; "but settle thyself where thou wilt; those of my calling are more becomingly employed in watching than in sleeping; still it would be as well if thou wert to dress this ear for me again, for it is giving me more pain than it need."

Sancho did as he bade him, but one of the goatherds, seeing the wound, told him not to be uneasy, as he would apply a remedy with which it would be soon healed; and gathering some leaves of rosemary, of which there was a great quantity there, he chewed them and mixed them with a little salt, and applying them to the ear he secured them firmly with a bandage, assuring him that no other treatment would be required, and so it proved.

CHAPTER XII.

OF WHAT A GOATHERD RELATED TO THOSE WITH DON QUIXOTE

Just then another young man, one of those who fetched their provisions from the village, came up and said, "Do you know what is going on in the village, comrades?"

"How could we know it?" replied one of them.

"Well, then, you must know," continued the young man, "this morning that famous student-shepherd called Chrysostom died, and it is rumoured that he died of love for that devil of a village girl the daughter of Guillermo the Rich, she that wanders about the wolds here in the dress of a shepherdess."

"You mean Marcela?" said one.

"Her I mean," answered the goatherd; "and the best of it is, he has directed in his will that he is to be buried in the fields like a Moor, and at the foot of the rock where the Cork-tree spring is, because, as the story goes (and they say he himself said so), that was the place where he first saw her. And he has also left other directions which the clergy of the village say should not and must not be obeyed because they savour of paganism. To all which his great friend Ambrosio the student, he who, like him, also went dressed as a shepherd, replies that everything must be done without any omission according to the directions left by Chrysostom, and about this the village is all in commotion; however, report says that, after all, what Ambrosio and all the shepherds his friends desire will be done, and to-morrow they are coming to bury him with great ceremony where I said. I am sure it will be something worth seeing; at least I will not fail to go and see it even if I knew I should not return to the village tomorrow."

"We will do the same," answered the goatherds, "and cast lots to see who must stay to mind the goats of all."

"Thou sayest well, Pedro," said one, "though there will be no need of taking that trouble, for I will stay behind for all; and don't suppose it is virtue or want of curiosity in me; it is that the splinter that ran into my foot the other day will not let me walk."

"For all that, we thank thee," answered Pedro.

Don Quixote asked Pedro to tell him who the dead man was and who the shepherdess, to which Pedro replied that all he knew was that the dead man was a wealthy gentleman belonging to a village in those mountains, who had been a student at Salamanca for many years, at the end of which he returned to his village with the reputation of being very learned and deeply read. "Above all, they said, he was learned in the science of the stars and of what went on yonder in the heavens and the sun and the moon, for he told us of the cris of the sun and moon to exact time."

"Eclipse it is called, friend, not cris, the darkening of those two luminaries," said Don Quixote; but Pedro, not troubling himself with trifles, went on with his story, saying, "Also he foretold when the year was going to be one of abundance or estility."

"Sterility, you mean," said Don Quixote.

"Sterility or estility," answered Pedro, "it is all the same in the end. And I can tell you that by this his father and friends who believed him grew very rich because they did as he advised them, bidding them 'sow barley this year, not wheat; this year you may sow pulse and not barley; the next there will be a full oil crop, and the three following not a drop will be got.'"

"That science is called astrology," said Don Quixote.

"I do not know what it is called," replied Pedro, "but I know that he knew all this and more besides. But, to make an end, not many months had passed after he returned from Salamanca, when one day he appeared dressed as a shepherd with his crook and sheepskin, having put off the long gown he wore as a scholar; and at the same time his great friend, Ambrosio by name, who had been his companion in his studies, took to the shepherd's dress with him. I forgot to say that Chrysostom, who is dead, was a great man for writing verses, so much so that he made carols for Christmas Eve, and plays for Corpus Christi, which the young men of our village acted, and all said they were excellent. When the villagers saw the two scholars so unexpectedly appearing in shepherd's dress, they were lost in wonder, and could not guess what had led them to make so extraordinary a change. About this time the father of our Chrysostom died, and he was left heir to a large amount of property in chattels as well as in land, no small number of cattle and sheep, and a large sum of money, of all of which the young man was left dissolute owner, and indeed he was deserving of it all, for he was a very good comrade, and kind-hearted, and a friend of worthy folk, and had a countenance like a benediction. Presently it came to be known that he had changed his dress with no other object than to wander about these wastes after that shepherdess Marcela our lad mentioned a while ago, with whom the deceased Chrysostom had fallen in love. And I must tell you now, for it is well you should know it, who this girl is; perhaps, and even without any perhaps, you will not have heard anything like it all the days of your life, though you should live more years than sarna."

"Say Sarra," said Don Quixote, unable to endure the goatherd's confusion of words.

"The sarna lives long enough," answered Pedro; "and if, senor, you must go finding fault with words at every step, we shall not make an end of it this twelvemonth."

"Pardon me, friend," said Don Quixote; "but, as there is such a difference between sarna and Sarra, I told you of it; however, you have answered very rightly, for sarna lives longer than Sarra: so continue your story, and I will not object any more to anything."

"I say then, my dear sir," said the goatherd, "that in our village there was a farmer even richer than the father of Chrysostom, who was named Guillermo, and upon whom God bestowed, over and above great wealth, a daughter at whose birth her mother died, the most respected woman there was in this neighbourhood; I fancy I can see her now with that countenance which had the sun on one side and the moon on the other; and moreover active, and kind to the poor, for which I trust that at the present moment her soul is in bliss with God in the other world. Her husband Guillermo died of grief at the death of so good a wife, leaving his daughter Marcela, a child and rich, to the care of an uncle of hers, a priest and prebendary in our village. The girl grew up with such beauty that it reminded us of her mother's, which was very great, and yet it was thought that the daughter's would exceed it; and so when she reached the age of fourteen to fifteen years nobody beheld her but blessed God that had made her so beautiful, and the greater number were in love with her past redemption. Her uncle kept her in great seclusion and retirement, but for all that the fame of her great beauty spread so that, as well for it as for her great wealth, her uncle was asked, solicited, and importuned, to give her in marriage not only by those of our town but of those many leagues round, and by the persons of highest quality in them. But he, being a good Christian man, though he desired to give her in marriage at once, seeing her to be old enough, was unwilling to do so without her consent, not that he had any eye to the gain and profit which the custody of the girl's property brought him while he put off her marriage; and, faith, this was said in praise of the good priest in more than one set in the town. For I would have you know, Sir Errant, that in these little villages everything is talked about and everything is carped at, and rest assured, as I am, that the priest must be over and above good who forces his parishioners to speak well of him, especially in villages."

"That is the truth," said Don Quixote; "but go on, for the story is very good, and you, good Pedro, tell it with very good grace."

"May that of the Lord not be wanting to me," said Pedro; "that is the one to have. To proceed; you must know that though the uncle put before his niece and described to her the qualities of each one in particular of the many who had asked her in marriage, begging her to marry and make a choice according to her own taste, she never gave any other answer than that she had no desire to marry just yet, and that being so young she did not think herself fit to bear the burden of matrimony. At these, to all appearance, reasonable excuses that she made, her uncle ceased to urge her, and waited till she was somewhat more advanced in age and could mate herself to her own liking. For, said he—and he said quite right—parents are not to settle children in life against their will. But when one least looked for it, lo and behold! one day the demure Marcela makes her appearance turned shepherdess; and, in spite of her uncle and all those of the town that strove to dissuade her, took to going a-field with the other shepherd-lasses of the village, and tending her own flock. And so, since she appeared in public, and her beauty came to be seen openly, I could not well tell you how many rich youths, gentlemen and peasants, have adopted the costume of Chrysostom, and go about these fields making love to her. One of these, as has been already said, was our deceased friend, of whom they say that he did not love but adore her. But you must not suppose, because Marcela chose a life of such liberty and independence, and of so little or rather no retirement, that she has given any occasion, or even the semblance of one, for disparagement of her purity and modesty; on the contrary, such and so great is the vigilance with which she watches over her honour, that of all those that court and woo her not one has boasted, or can with truth boast, that she has given him any hope however small of obtaining his desire. For although she does not avoid or shun the society and conversation of the shepherds, and treats them courteously and kindly, should any one of them come to declare his intention to her, though it be one as proper and holy as that of matrimony, she flings him from her like a catapult. And with this kind of disposition she does more harm in this country than if the plague had got into it, for her affability and her beauty draw on the hearts of those that associate with her to love her and to court her, but her scorn and her frankness bring them to the brink of despair; and so they know not what to say save to proclaim her aloud cruel and hard-hearted, and other names of the same sort which well describe the nature of her character; and if you should remain here any time, senor, you would hear these hills and valleys resounding with the laments of the rejected ones who pursue her. Not far from this there is a spot where there are a couple of dozen of tall beeches, and there is not one of them but has carved and written on its smooth bark the name of Marcela, and above some a crown carved on the same tree as though her lover would say more plainly that Marcela wore and deserved that of all human beauty. Here one shepherd is sighing, there another is lamenting; there love songs are heard, here despairing elegies. One will pass all the hours of the night seated at the foot of some oak or rock, and there, without having closed his weeping eyes, the sun finds him in the morning bemused and bereft of sense; and another without relief or respite to his sighs, stretched on the burning sand in the full heat of the sultry summer noontide, makes his appeal to the compassionate heavens, and over one and the other, over these and all, the beautiful Marcela triumphs free and careless. And all of us that know her are waiting to see what her pride will come to, and who is to be the happy man that will succeed in taming a nature so formidable and gaining possession of a beauty so supreme. All that I have told you being such well-established truth, I am persuaded that what they say of the cause of Chrysostom's death, as our lad told us, is the same. And so I advise you, senor, fail not to be present to-morrow at his burial, which will be well worth seeing, for Chrysostom had many friends, and it is not half a league from this place to where he directed he should be buried."

"I will make a point of it," said Don Quixote, "and I thank you for the pleasure you have given me by relating so interesting a tale."

"Oh," said the goatherd, "I do not know even the half of what has happened to the lovers of Marcela, but perhaps to-morrow we may fall in with some shepherd on the road who can tell us; and now it will be well for you to go and sleep under cover, for the night air may hurt your wound, though with the remedy I have applied to you there is no fear of an untoward result."

Sancho Panza, who was wishing the goatherd's loquacity at the devil, on his part begged his master to go into Pedro's hut to sleep. He did so, and passed all the rest of the night in thinking of his lady Dulcinea, in imitation of the lovers of Marcela. Sancho Panza settled himself between Rocinante and his ass, and slept, not like a lover who had been discarded, but like a man who had been soundly kicked.

CHAPTER XIII.

IN WHICH IS ENDED THE STORY OF THE SHEPHERDESS MARCELA, WITH OTHER INCIDENTS

Bit hardly had day begun to show itself through the balconies of the east, when five of the six goatherds came to rouse Don Quixote and tell him that if he was still of a mind to go and see the famous burial of Chrysostom they would bear him company. Don Quixote, who desired nothing better, rose and ordered Sancho to saddle and pannel at once, which he did with all despatch, and with the same they all set out forthwith. They had not gone a quarter of a league when at the meeting of two paths they saw coming towards them some six shepherds dressed in black sheepskins and with their heads crowned with garlands of cypress and bitter oleander. Each of them carried a stout holly staff in his hand, and along with them there came two men of quality on horseback in handsome travelling dress, with three servants on foot accompanying them. Courteous salutations were exchanged on meeting, and inquiring one of the other which way each party was going, they learned that all were bound for the scene of the burial, so they went on all together.

One of those on horseback addressing his companion said to him, "It seems to me, Senor Vivaldo, that we may reckon as well spent the delay we shall incur in seeing this remarkable funeral, for remarkable it cannot but be judging by the strange things these shepherds have told us, of both the dead shepherd and homicide shepherdess."

"So I think too," replied Vivaldo, "and I would delay not to say a day, but four, for the sake of seeing it."

Don Quixote asked them what it was they had heard of Marcela and Chrysostom. The traveller answered that the same morning they had met these shepherds, and seeing them dressed in this mournful fashion they had asked them the reason of their appearing in such a guise; which one of them gave, describing the strange behaviour and beauty of a shepherdess called Marcela, and the loves of many who courted her, together with the death of that Chrysostom to whose burial they were going. In short, he repeated all that Pedro had related to Don Quixote.

This conversation dropped, and another was commenced by him who was called Vivaldo asking Don Quixote what was the reason that led him to go armed in that fashion in a country so peaceful. To which Don Quixote replied, "The pursuit of my calling does not allow or permit me to go in any other fashion; easy life, enjoyment, and repose were invented for soft courtiers, but toil, unrest, and arms were invented and made for those alone whom the world calls knights-errant, of whom I, though unworthy, am the least of all."

The instant they heard this all set him down as mad, and the better to settle the point and discover what kind of madness his was, Vivaldo proceeded to ask him what knights-errant meant.

"Have not your worships," replied Don Quixote, "read the annals and histories of England, in which are recorded the famous deeds of King Arthur, whom we in our popular Castilian invariably call King Artus, with regard to whom it is an ancient tradition, and commonly received all over that kingdom of Great Britain, that this king did not die, but was changed by magic art into a raven, and that in process of time he is to return to reign and recover his kingdom and sceptre; for which reason it cannot be proved that from that time to this any Englishman ever killed a raven? Well, then, in the time of this good king that famous order of chivalry of the Knights of the Round Table was instituted, and the amour of Don Lancelot of the Lake with the Queen Guinevere occurred, precisely as is there related, the go-between and confidante therein being the highly honourable dame Quintanona, whence came that ballad so well known and widely spread in our Spain—

O never surely was there knight

  So served by hand of dame,

As served was he Sir Lancelot hight

  When he from Britain came—

with all the sweet and delectable course of his achievements in love and war. Handed down from that time, then, this order of chivalry went on extending and spreading itself over many and various parts of the world; and in it, famous and renowned for their deeds, were the mighty Amadis of Gaul with all his sons and descendants to the fifth generation, and the valiant Felixmarte of Hircania, and the never sufficiently praised Tirante el Blanco, and in our own days almost we have seen and heard and talked with the invincible knight Don Belianis of Greece. This, then, sirs, is to be a knight-errant, and what I have spoken of is the order of his chivalry, of which, as I have already said, I, though a sinner, have made profession, and what the aforesaid knights professed that same do I profess, and so I go through these solitudes and wilds seeking adventures, resolved in soul to oppose my arm and person to the most perilous that fortune may offer me in aid of the weak and needy."

By these words of his the travellers were able to satisfy themselves of Don Quixote's being out of his senses and of the form of madness that overmastered him, at which they felt the same astonishment that all felt on first becoming acquainted with it; and Vivaldo, who was a person of great shrewdness and of a lively temperament, in order to beguile the short journey which they said was required to reach the mountain, the scene of the burial, sought to give him an opportunity of going on with his absurdities. So he said to him, "It seems to me, Senor Knight-errant, that your worship has made choice of one of the most austere professions in the world, and I imagine even that of the Carthusian monks is not so austere."

"As austere it may perhaps be," replied our Don Quixote, "but so necessary for the world I am very much inclined to doubt. For, if the truth is to be told, the soldier who executes what his captain orders does no less than the captain himself who gives the order. My meaning, is, that churchmen in peace and quiet pray to Heaven for the welfare of the world, but we soldiers and knights carry into effect what they pray for, defending it with the might of our arms and the edge of our swords, not under shelter but in the open air, a target for the intolerable rays of the sun in summer and the piercing frosts of winter. Thus are we God's ministers on earth and the arms by which his justice is done therein. And as the business of war and all that relates and belongs to it cannot be conducted without exceeding great sweat, toil, and exertion, it follows that those who make it their profession have undoubtedly more labour than those who in tranquil peace and quiet are engaged in praying to God to help the weak. I do not mean to say, nor does it enter into my thoughts, that the knight-errant's calling is as good as that of the monk in his cell; I would merely infer from what I endure myself that it is beyond a doubt a more laborious and a more belaboured one, a hungrier and thirstier, a wretcheder, raggeder, and lousier; for there is no reason to doubt that the knights-errant of yore endured much hardship in the course of their lives. And if some of them by the might of their arms did rise to be emperors, in faith it cost them dear in the matter of blood and sweat; and if those who attained to that rank had not had magicians and sages to help them they would have been completely baulked in their ambition and disappointed in their hopes."

"That is my own opinion," replied the traveller; "but one thing among many others seems to me very wrong in knights-errant, and that is that when they find themselves about to engage in some mighty and perilous adventure in which there is manifest danger of losing their lives, they never at the moment of engaging in it think of commending themselves to God, as is the duty of every good Christian in like peril; instead of which they commend themselves to their ladies with as much devotion as if these were their gods, a thing which seems to me to savour somewhat of heathenism."

"Sir," answered Don Quixote, "that cannot be on any account omitted, and the knight-errant would be disgraced who acted otherwise: for it is usual and customary in knight-errantry that the knight-errant, who on engaging in any great feat of arms has his lady before him, should turn his eyes towards her softly and lovingly, as though with them entreating her to favour and protect him in the hazardous venture he is about to undertake, and even though no one hear him, he is bound to say certain words between his teeth, commending himself to her with all his heart, and of this we have innumerable instances in the histories. Nor is it to be supposed from this that they are to omit commending themselves to God, for there will be time and opportunity for doing so while they are engaged in their task."

"For all that," answered the traveller, "I feel some doubt still, because often I have read how words will arise between two knights-errant, and from one thing to another it comes about that their anger kindles and they wheel their horses round and take a good stretch of field, and then without any more ado at the top of their speed they come to the charge, and in mid-career they are wont to commend themselves to their ladies; and what commonly comes of the encounter is that one falls over the haunches of his horse pierced through and through by his antagonist's lance, and as for the other, it is only by holding on to the mane of his horse that he can help falling to the ground; but I know not how the dead man had time to commend himself to God in the course of such rapid work as this; it would have been better if those words which he spent in commending himself to his lady in the midst of his career had been devoted to his duty and obligation as a Christian. Moreover, it is my belief that all knights-errant have not ladies to commend themselves to, for they are not all in love."

"That is impossible," said Don Quixote: "I say it is impossible that there could be a knight-errant without a lady, because to such it is as natural and proper to be in love as to the heavens to have stars: most certainly no history has been seen in which there is to be found a knight-errant without an amour, and for the simple reason that without one he would be held no legitimate knight but a bastard, and one who had gained entrance into the stronghold of the said knighthood, not by the door, but over the wall like a thief and a robber."

"Nevertheless," said the traveller, "if I remember rightly, I think I have read that Don Galaor, the brother of the valiant Amadis of Gaul, never had any special lady to whom he might commend himself, and yet he was not the less esteemed, and was a very stout and famous knight."

To which our Don Quixote made answer, "Sir, one solitary swallow does not make summer; moreover, I know that knight was in secret very deeply in love; besides which, that way of falling in love with all that took his fancy was a natural propensity which he could not control. But, in short, it is very manifest that he had one alone whom he made mistress of his will, to whom he commended himself very frequently and very secretly, for he prided himself on being a reticent knight."

"Then if it be essential that every knight-errant should be in love," said the traveller, "it may be fairly supposed that your worship is so, as you are of the order; and if you do not pride yourself on being as reticent as Don Galaor, I entreat you as earnestly as I can, in the name of all this company and in my own, to inform us of the name, country, rank, and beauty of your lady, for she will esteem herself fortunate if all the world knows that she is loved and served by such a knight as your worship seems to be."

At this Don Quixote heaved a deep sigh and said, "I cannot say positively whether my sweet enemy is pleased or not that the world should know I serve her; I can only say in answer to what has been so courteously asked of me, that her name is Dulcinea, her country El Toboso, a village of La Mancha, her rank must be at least that of a princess, since she is my queen and lady, and her beauty superhuman, since all the impossible and fanciful attributes of beauty which the poets apply to their ladies are verified in her; for her hairs are gold, her forehead Elysian fields, her eyebrows rainbows, her eyes suns, her cheeks roses, her lips coral, her teeth pearls, her neck alabaster, her bosom marble, her hands ivory, her fairness snow, and what modesty conceals from sight such, I think and imagine, as rational reflection can only extol, not compare."

"We should like to know her lineage, race, and ancestry," said Vivaldo.

To which Don Quixote replied, "She is not of the ancient Roman Curtii, Caii, or Scipios, nor of the modern Colonnas or Orsini, nor of the Moncadas or Requesenes of Catalonia, nor yet of the Rebellas or Villanovas of Valencia; Palafoxes, Nuzas, Rocabertis, Corellas, Lunas, Alagones, Urreas, Foces, or Gurreas of Aragon; Cerdas, Manriques, Mendozas, or Guzmans of Castile; Alencastros, Pallas, or Meneses of Portugal; but she is of those of El Toboso of La Mancha, a lineage that though modern, may furnish a source of gentle blood for the most illustrious families of the ages that are to come, and this let none dispute with me save on the condition that Zerbino placed at the foot of the trophy of Orlando's arms, saying,

'These let none move Who dareth not his might with Roland prove.'"

"Although mine is of the Cachopins of Laredo," said the traveller, "I will not venture to compare it with that of El Toboso of La Mancha, though, to tell the truth, no such surname has until now ever reached my ears."

"What!" said Don Quixote, "has that never reached them?"

The rest of the party went along listening with great attention to the conversation of the pair, and even the very goatherds and shepherds perceived how exceedingly out of his wits our Don Quixote was. Sancho Panza alone thought that what his master said was the truth, knowing who he was and having known him from his birth; and all that he felt any difficulty in believing was that about the fair Dulcinea del Toboso, because neither any such name nor any such princess had ever come to his knowledge though he lived so close to El Toboso. They were going along conversing in this way, when they saw descending a gap between two high mountains some twenty shepherds, all clad in sheepskins of black wool, and crowned with garlands which, as afterwards appeared, were, some of them of yew, some of cypress. Six of the number were carrying a bier covered with a great variety of flowers and branches, on seeing which one of the goatherds said, "Those who come there are the bearers of Chrysostom's body, and the foot of that mountain is the place where he ordered them to bury him." They therefore made haste to reach the spot, and did so by the time those who came had laid the bier upon the ground, and four of them with sharp pickaxes were digging a grave by the side of a hard rock. They greeted each other courteously, and then Don Quixote and those who accompanied him turned to examine the bier, and on it, covered with flowers, they saw a dead body in the dress of a shepherd, to all appearance of one thirty years of age, and showing even in death that in life he had been of comely features and gallant bearing. Around him on the bier itself were laid some books, and several papers open and folded; and those who were looking on as well as those who were opening the grave and all the others who were there preserved a strange silence, until one of those who had borne the body said to another, "Observe carefully, Ambrosia if this is the place Chrysostom spoke of, since you are anxious that what he directed in his will should be so strictly complied with."

"This is the place," answered Ambrosia "for in it many a time did my poor friend tell me the story of his hard fortune. Here it was, he told me, that he saw for the first time that mortal enemy of the human race, and here, too, for the first time he declared to her his passion, as honourable as it was devoted, and here it was that at last Marcela ended by scorning and rejecting him so as to bring the tragedy of his wretched life to a close; here, in memory of misfortunes so great, he desired to be laid in the bowels of eternal oblivion." Then turning to Don Quixote and the travellers he went on to say, "That body, sirs, on which you are looking with compassionate eyes, was the abode of a soul on which Heaven bestowed a vast share of its riches. That is the body of Chrysostom, who was unrivalled in wit, unequalled in courtesy, unapproached in gentle bearing, a phoenix in friendship, generous without limit, grave without arrogance, gay without vulgarity, and, in short, first in all that constitutes goodness and second to none in all that makes up misfortune. He loved deeply, he was hated; he adored, he was scorned; he wooed a wild beast, he pleaded with marble, he pursued the wind, he cried to the wilderness, he served ingratitude, and for reward was made the prey of death in the mid-course of life, cut short by a shepherdess whom he sought to immortalise in the memory of man, as these papers which you see could fully prove, had he not commanded me to consign them to the fire after having consigned his body to the earth."

"You would deal with them more harshly and cruelly than their owner himself," said Vivaldo, "for it is neither right nor proper to do the will of one who enjoins what is wholly unreasonable; it would not have been reasonable in Augustus Caesar had he permitted the directions left by the divine Mantuan in his will to be carried into effect. So that, Senor Ambrosia while you consign your friend's body to the earth, you should not consign his writings to oblivion, for if he gave the order in bitterness of heart, it is not right that you should irrationally obey it. On the contrary, by granting life to those papers, let the cruelty of Marcela live for ever, to serve as a warning in ages to come to all men to shun and avoid falling into like danger; or I and all of us who have come here know already the story of this your love-stricken and heart-broken friend, and we know, too, your friendship, and the cause of his death, and the directions he gave at the close of his life; from which sad story may be gathered how great was the cruelty of Marcela, the love of Chrysostom, and the loyalty of your friendship, together with the end awaiting those who pursue rashly the path that insane passion opens to their eyes. Last night we learned the death of Chrysostom and that he was to be buried here, and out of curiosity and pity we left our direct road and resolved to come and see with our eyes that which when heard of had so moved our compassion, and in consideration of that compassion and our desire to prove it if we might by condolence, we beg of you, excellent Ambrosia, or at least I on my own account entreat you, that instead of burning those papers you allow me to carry away some of them."

And without waiting for the shepherd's answer, he stretched out his hand and took up some of those that were nearest to him; seeing which Ambrosio said, "Out of courtesy, senor, I will grant your request as to those you have taken, but it is idle to expect me to abstain from burning the remainder."

Vivaldo, who was eager to see what the papers contained, opened one of them at once, and saw that its title was "Lay of Despair."

Ambrosio hearing it said, "That is the last paper the unhappy man wrote; and that you may see, senor, to what an end his misfortunes brought him, read it so that you may be heard, for you will have time enough for that while we are waiting for the grave to be dug."

"I will do so very willingly," said Vivaldo; and as all the bystanders were equally eager they gathered round him, and he, reading in a loud voice, found that it ran as follows.

CHAPTER XIV.

WHEREIN ARE INSERTED THE DESPAIRING VERSES OF THE DEAD SHEPHERD, TOGETHER WITH OTHER INCIDENTS NOT LOOKED FOR

THE LAY OF CHRYSOSTOM

  Since thou dost in thy cruelty desire

The ruthless rigour of thy tyranny

From tongue to tongue, from land to land proclaimed,

The very Hell will I constrain to lend

This stricken breast of mine deep notes of woe

To serve my need of fitting utterance.

And as I strive to body forth the tale

Of all I suffer, all that thou hast done,

Forth shall the dread voice roll, and bear along

Shreds from my vitals torn for greater pain.

Then listen, not to dulcet harmony,

But to a discord wrung by mad despair

Out of this bosom's depths of bitterness,

To ease my heart and plant a sting in thine.

The lion's roar, the fierce wolf's savage howl,

The horrid hissing of the scaly snake,

The awesome cries of monsters yet unnamed,

The crow's ill-boding croak, the hollow moan

Of wild winds wrestling with the restless sea,

The wrathful bellow of the vanquished bull,

The plaintive sobbing of the widowed dove,

The envied owl's sad note, the wail of woe

That rises from the dreary choir of Hell,

Commingled in one sound, confusing sense,

Let all these come to aid my soul's complaint,

For pain like mine demands new modes of song.

No echoes of that discord shall be heard

Where Father Tagus rolls, or on the banks

Of olive-bordered Betis; to the rocks

Or in deep caverns shall my plaint be told,

And by a lifeless tongue in living words;

Or in dark valleys or on lonely shores,

Where neither foot of man nor sunbeam falls;

Or in among the poison-breathing swarms

Of monsters nourished by the sluggish Nile.

For, though it be to solitudes remote

The hoarse vague echoes of my sorrows sound

Thy matchless cruelty, my dismal fate

Shall carry them to all the spacious world.

Disdain hath power to kill, and patience dies

Slain by suspicion, be it false or true;

And deadly is the force of jealousy;

Long absence makes of life a dreary void;

No hope of happiness can give repose

To him that ever fears to be forgot;

And death, inevitable, waits in hall.

But I, by some strange miracle, live on

A prey to absence, jealousy, disdain;

Racked by suspicion as by certainty;

Forgotten, left to feed my flame alone.

And while I suffer thus, there comes no ray

Of hope to gladden me athwart the gloom;

Nor do I look for it in my despair;

But rather clinging to a cureless woe,

All hope do I abjure for evermore.

Can there be hope where fear is? Were it well,

When far more certain are the grounds of fear?

Ought I to shut mine eyes to jealousy,

If through a thousand heart-wounds it appears?

Who would not give free access to distrust,

Seeing disdain unveiled, and—bitter change!—

All his suspicions turned to certainties,

And the fair truth transformed into a lie?

Oh, thou fierce tyrant of the realms of love,

Oh, Jealousy! put chains upon these hands,

And bind me with thy strongest cord, Disdain.

But, woe is me! triumphant over all,

My sufferings drown the memory of you.

And now I die, and since there is no hope

Of happiness for me in life or death,

Still to my fantasy I'll fondly cling.

I'll say that he is wise who loveth well,

And that the soul most free is that most bound

In thraldom to the ancient tyrant Love.

I'll say that she who is mine enemy

In that fair body hath as fair a mind,

And that her coldness is but my desert,

And that by virtue of the pain he sends

Love rules his kingdom with a gentle sway.

Thus, self-deluding, and in bondage sore,

And wearing out the wretched shred of life

To which I am reduced by her disdain,

I'll give this soul and body to the winds,

All hopeless of a crown of bliss in store.

Thou whose injustice hath supplied the cause

That makes me quit the weary life I loathe,

As by this wounded bosom thou canst see

How willingly thy victim I become,

Let not my death, if haply worth a tear,

Cloud the clear heaven that dwells in thy bright eyes;

I would not have thee expiate in aught

The crime of having made my heart thy prey;

But rather let thy laughter gaily ring

And prove my death to be thy festival.

Fool that I am to bid thee! well I know

Thy glory gains by my untimely end.

And now it is the time; from Hell's abyss

Come thirsting Tantalus, come Sisyphus

Heaving the cruel stone, come Tityus

With vulture, and with wheel Ixion come,

And come the sisters of the ceaseless toil;

And all into this breast transfer their pains,

And (if such tribute to despair be due)

Chant in their deepest tones a doleful dirge

Over a corse unworthy of a shroud.

Let the three-headed guardian of the gate,

And all the monstrous progeny of hell,

The doleful concert join: a lover dead

Methinks can have no fitter obsequies.

  Lay of despair, grieve not when thou art gone

Forth from this sorrowing heart: my misery

Brings fortune to the cause that gave thee birth;

Then banish sadness even in the tomb.

The "Lay of Chrysostom" met with the approbation of the listeners, though the reader said it did not seem to him to agree with what he had heard of Marcela's reserve and propriety, for Chrysostom complained in it of jealousy, suspicion, and absence, all to the prejudice of the good name and fame of Marcela; to which Ambrosio replied as one who knew well his friend's most secret thoughts, "Senor, to remove that doubt I should tell you that when the unhappy man wrote this lay he was away from Marcela, from whom he had voluntarily separated himself, to try if absence would act with him as it is wont; and as everything distresses and every fear haunts the banished lover, so imaginary jealousies and suspicions, dreaded as if they were true, tormented Chrysostom; and thus the truth of what report declares of the virtue of Marcela remains unshaken, and with her envy itself should not and cannot find any fault save that of being cruel, somewhat haughty, and very scornful."

"That is true," said Vivaldo; and as he was about to read another paper of those he had preserved from the fire, he was stopped by a marvellous vision (for such it seemed) that unexpectedly presented itself to their eyes; for on the summit of the rock where they were digging the grave there appeared the shepherdess Marcela, so beautiful that her beauty exceeded its reputation. Those who had never till then beheld her gazed upon her in wonder and silence, and those who were accustomed to see her were not less amazed than those who had never seen her before. But the instant Ambrosio saw her he addressed her, with manifest indignation:

"Art thou come, by chance, cruel basilisk of these mountains, to see if in thy presence blood will flow from the wounds of this wretched being thy cruelty has robbed of life; or is it to exult over the cruel work of thy humours that thou art come; or like another pitiless Nero to look down from that height upon the ruin of his Rome in embers; or in thy arrogance to trample on this ill-fated corpse, as the ungrateful daughter trampled on her father Tarquin's? Tell us quickly for what thou art come, or what it is thou wouldst have, for, as I know the thoughts of Chrysostom never failed to obey thee in life, I will make all these who call themselves his friends obey thee, though he be dead."

"I come not, Ambrosia for any of the purposes thou hast named," replied Marcela, "but to defend myself and to prove how unreasonable are all those who blame me for their sorrow and for Chrysostom's death; and therefore I ask all of you that are here to give me your attention, for will not take much time or many words to bring the truth home to persons of sense. Heaven has made me, so you say, beautiful, and so much so that in spite of yourselves my beauty leads you to love me; and for the love you show me you say, and even urge, that I am bound to love you. By that natural understanding which God has given me I know that everything beautiful attracts love, but I cannot see how, by reason of being loved, that which is loved for its beauty is bound to love that which loves it; besides, it may happen that the lover of that which is beautiful may be ugly, and ugliness being detestable, it is very absurd to say, "I love thee because thou art beautiful, thou must love me though I be ugly." But supposing the beauty equal on both sides, it does not follow that the inclinations must be therefore alike, for it is not every beauty that excites love, some but pleasing the eye without winning the affection; and if every sort of beauty excited love and won the heart, the will would wander vaguely to and fro unable to make choice of any; for as there is an infinity of beautiful objects there must be an infinity of inclinations, and true love, I have heard it said, is indivisible, and must be voluntary and not compelled. If this be so, as I believe it to be, why do you desire me to bend my will by force, for no other reason but that you say you love me? Nay—tell me—had Heaven made me ugly, as it has made me beautiful, could I with justice complain of you for not loving me? Moreover, you must remember that the beauty I possess was no choice of mine, for, be it what it may, Heaven of its bounty gave it me without my asking or choosing it; and as the viper, though it kills with it, does not deserve to be blamed for the poison it carries, as it is a gift of nature, neither do I deserve reproach for being beautiful; for beauty in a modest woman is like fire at a distance or a sharp sword; the one does not burn, the other does not cut, those who do not come too near. Honour and virtue are the ornaments of the mind, without which the body, though it be so, has no right to pass for beautiful; but if modesty is one of the virtues that specially lend a grace and charm to mind and body, why should she who is loved for her beauty part with it to gratify one who for his pleasure alone strives with all his might and energy to rob her of it? I was born free, and that I might live in freedom I chose the solitude of the fields; in the trees of the mountains I find society, the clear waters of the brooks are my mirrors, and to the trees and waters I make known my thoughts and charms. I am a fire afar off, a sword laid aside. Those whom I have inspired with love by letting them see me, I have by words undeceived, and if their longings live on hope—and I have given none to Chrysostom or to any other—it cannot justly be said that the death of any is my doing, for it was rather his own obstinacy than my cruelty that killed him; and if it be made a charge against me that his wishes were honourable, and that therefore I was bound to yield to them, I answer that when on this very spot where now his grave is made he declared to me his purity of purpose, I told him that mine was to live in perpetual solitude, and that the earth alone should enjoy the fruits of my retirement and the spoils of my beauty; and if, after this open avowal, he chose to persist against hope and steer against the wind, what wonder is it that he should sink in the depths of his infatuation? If I had encouraged him, I should be false; if I had gratified him, I should have acted against my own better resolution and purpose. He was persistent in spite of warning, he despaired without being hated. Bethink you now if it be reasonable that his suffering should be laid to my charge. Let him who has been deceived complain, let him give way to despair whose encouraged hopes have proved vain, let him flatter himself whom I shall entice, let him boast whom I shall receive; but let not him call me cruel or homicide to whom I make no promise, upon whom I practise no deception, whom I neither entice nor receive. It has not been so far the will of Heaven that I should love by fate, and to expect me to love by choice is idle. Let this general declaration serve for each of my suitors on his own account, and let it be understood from this time forth that if anyone dies for me it is not of jealousy or misery he dies, for she who loves no one can give no cause for jealousy to any, and candour is not to be confounded with scorn. Let him who calls me wild beast and basilisk, leave me alone as something noxious and evil; let him who calls me ungrateful, withhold his service; who calls me wayward, seek not my acquaintance; who calls me cruel, pursue me not; for this wild beast, this basilisk, this ungrateful, cruel, wayward being has no kind of desire to seek, serve, know, or follow them. If Chrysostom's impatience and violent passion killed him, why should my modest behaviour and circumspection be blamed? If I preserve my purity in the society of the trees, why should he who would have me preserve it among men, seek to rob me of it? I have, as you know, wealth of my own, and I covet not that of others; my taste is for freedom, and I have no relish for constraint; I neither love nor hate anyone; I do not deceive this one or court that, or trifle with one or play with another. The modest converse of the shepherd girls of these hamlets and the care of my goats are my recreations; my desires are bounded by these mountains, and if they ever wander hence it is to contemplate the beauty of the heavens, steps by which the soul travels to its primeval abode."

With these words, and not waiting to hear a reply, she turned and passed into the thickest part of a wood that was hard by, leaving all who were there lost in admiration as much of her good sense as of her beauty. Some—those wounded by the irresistible shafts launched by her bright eyes—made as though they would follow her, heedless of the frank declaration they had heard; seeing which, and deeming this a fitting occasion for the exercise of his chivalry in aid of distressed damsels, Don Quixote, laying his hand on the hilt of his sword, exclaimed in a loud and distinct voice:

"Let no one, whatever his rank or condition, dare to follow the beautiful Marcela, under pain of incurring my fierce indignation. She has shown by clear and satisfactory arguments that little or no fault is to be found with her for the death of Chrysostom, and also how far she is from yielding to the wishes of any of her lovers, for which reason, instead of being followed and persecuted, she should in justice be honoured and esteemed by all the good people of the world, for she shows that she is the only woman in it that holds to such a virtuous resolution."

Whether it was because of the threats of Don Quixote, or because Ambrosio told them to fulfil their duty to their good friend, none of the shepherds moved or stirred from the spot until, having finished the grave and burned Chrysostom's papers, they laid his body in it, not without many tears from those who stood by. They closed the grave with a heavy stone until a slab was ready which Ambrosio said he meant to have prepared, with an epitaph which was to be to this effect:

Beneath the stone before your eyes

The body of a lover lies;

In life he was a shepherd swain,

In death a victim to disdain.

Ungrateful, cruel, coy, and fair,

Was she that drove him to despair,

And Love hath made her his ally

For spreading wide his tyranny.

They then strewed upon the grave a profusion of flowers and branches, and all expressing their condolence with his friend ambrosio, took their Vivaldo and his companion did the same; and Don Quixote bade farewell to his hosts and to the travellers, who pressed him to come with them to Seville, as being such a convenient place for finding adventures, for they presented themselves in every street and round every corner oftener than anywhere else. Don Quixote thanked them for their advice and for the disposition they showed to do him a favour, and said that for the present he would not, and must not go to Seville until he had cleared all these mountains of highwaymen and robbers, of whom report said they were full. Seeing his good intention, the travellers were unwilling to press him further, and once more bidding him farewell, they left him and pursued their journey, in the course of which they did not fail to discuss the story of Marcela and Chrysostom as well as the madness of Don Quixote. He, on his part, resolved to go in quest of the shepherdess Marcela, and make offer to her of all the service he could render her; but things did not fall out with him as he expected, according to what is related in the course of this veracious history, of which the Second Part ends here.

CHAPTER XV.

IN WHICH IS RELATED THE UNFORTUNATE ADVENTURE THAT DON QUIXOTE FELL IN WITH WHEN HE FELL OUT WITH CERTAIN HEARTLESS YANGUESANS

The sage Cide Hamete Benengeli relates that as soon as Don Quixote took leave of his hosts and all who had been present at the burial of Chrysostom, he and his squire passed into the same wood which they had seen the shepherdess Marcela enter, and after having wandered for more than two hours in all directions in search of her without finding her, they came to a halt in a glade covered with tender grass, beside which ran a pleasant cool stream that invited and compelled them to pass there the hours of the noontide heat, which by this time was beginning to come on oppressively. Don Quixote and Sancho dismounted, and turning Rocinante and the ass loose to feed on the grass that was there in abundance, they ransacked the alforjas, and without any ceremony very peacefully and sociably master and man made their repast on what they found in them.

Sancho had not thought it worth while to hobble Rocinante, feeling sure, from what he knew of his staidness and freedom from incontinence, that all the mares in the Cordova pastures would not lead him into an impropriety. Chance, however, and the devil, who is not always asleep, so ordained it that feeding in this valley there was a drove of Galician ponies belonging to certain Yanguesan carriers, whose way it is to take their midday rest with their teams in places and spots where grass and water abound; and that where Don Quixote chanced to be suited the Yanguesans' purpose very well. It so happened, then, that Rocinante took a fancy to disport himself with their ladyships the ponies, and abandoning his usual gait and demeanour as he scented them, he, without asking leave of his master, got up a briskish little trot and hastened to make known his wishes to them; they, however, it seemed, preferred their pasture to him, and received him with their heels and teeth to such effect that they soon broke his girths and left him naked without a saddle to cover him; but what must have been worse to him was that the carriers, seeing the violence he was offering to their mares, came running up armed with stakes, and so belaboured him that they brought him sorely battered to the ground.

By this time Don Quixote and Sancho, who had witnessed the drubbing of

Rocinante, came up panting, and said Don Quixote to Sancho:

"So far as I can see, friend Sancho, these are not knights but base folk of low birth: I mention it because thou canst lawfully aid me in taking due vengeance for the insult offered to Rocinante before our eyes."

"What the devil vengeance can we take," answered Sancho, "if they are more than twenty, and we no more than two, or, indeed, perhaps not more than one and a half?"

"I count for a hundred," replied Don Quixote, and without more words he drew his sword and attacked the Yanguesans and excited and impelled by the example of his master, Sancho did the same; and to begin with, Don Quixote delivered a slash at one of them that laid open the leather jerkin he wore, together with a great portion of his shoulder. The Yanguesans, seeing themselves assaulted by only two men while they were so many, betook themselves to their stakes, and driving the two into the middle they began to lay on with great zeal and energy; in fact, at the second blow they brought Sancho to the ground, and Don Quixote fared the same way, all his skill and high mettle availing him nothing, and fate willed it that he should fall at the feet of Rocinante, who had not yet risen; whereby it may be seen how furiously stakes can pound in angry boorish hands.

Then, seeing the mischief they had done, the Yanguesans with all the haste they could loaded their team and pursued their journey, leaving the two adventurers a sorry sight and in sorrier mood.

Sancho was the first to come to, and finding himself close to his master he called to him in a weak and doleful voice, "Senor Don Quixote, ah, Senor Don Quixote!"

"What wouldst thou, brother Sancho?" answered Don Quixote in the same feeble suffering tone as Sancho.

"I would like, if it were possible," answered Sancho Panza, "your worship to give me a couple of sups of that potion of the fiery Blas, if it be that you have any to hand there; perhaps it will serve for broken bones as well as for wounds."

"If I only had it here, wretch that I am, what more should we want?" said Don Quixote; "but I swear to thee, Sancho Panza, on the faith of a knight-errant, ere two days are over, unless fortune orders otherwise, I mean to have it in my possession, or my hand will have lost its cunning."

"But in how many does your worship think we shall have the use of our feet?" answered Sancho Panza.

"For myself I must say I cannot guess how many," said the battered knight Don Quixote; "but I take all the blame upon myself, for I had no business to put hand to sword against men who where not dubbed knights like myself, and so I believe that in punishment for having transgressed the laws of chivalry the God of battles has permitted this chastisement to be administered to me; for which reason, brother Sancho, it is well thou shouldst receive a hint on the matter which I am now about to mention to thee, for it is of much importance to the welfare of both of us. It is at when thou shalt see rabble of this sort offering us insult thou art not to wait till I draw sword against them, for I shall not do so at all; but do thou draw sword and chastise them to thy heart's content, and if any knights come to their aid and defence I will take care to defend thee and assail them with all my might; and thou hast already seen by a thousand signs and proofs what the might of this strong arm of mine is equal to"—so uplifted had the poor gentleman become through the victory over the stout Biscayan.

But Sancho did not so fully approve of his master's admonition as to let it pass without saying in reply, "Senor, I am a man of peace, meek and quiet, and I can put up with any affront because I have a wife and children to support and bring up; so let it be likewise a hint to your worship, as it cannot be a mandate, that on no account will I draw sword either against clown or against knight, and that here before God I forgive the insults that have been offered me, whether they have been, are, or shall be offered me by high or low, rich or poor, noble or commoner, not excepting any rank or condition whatsoever."

To all which his master said in reply, "I wish I had breath enough to speak somewhat easily, and that the pain I feel on this side would abate so as to let me explain to thee, Panza, the mistake thou makest. Come now, sinner, suppose the wind of fortune, hitherto so adverse, should turn in our favour, filling the sails of our desires so that safely and without impediment we put into port in some one of those islands I have promised thee, how would it be with thee if on winning it I made thee lord of it? Why, thou wilt make it well-nigh impossible through not being a knight nor having any desire to be one, nor possessing the courage nor the will to avenge insults or defend thy lordship; for thou must know that in newly conquered kingdoms and provinces the minds of the inhabitants are never so quiet nor so well disposed to the new lord that there is no fear of their making some move to change matters once more, and try, as they say, what chance may do for them; so it is essential that the new possessor should have good sense to enable him to govern, and valour to attack and defend himself, whatever may befall him."

"In what has now befallen us," answered Sancho, "I'd have been well pleased to have that good sense and that valour your worship speaks of, but I swear on the faith of a poor man I am more fit for plasters than for arguments. See if your worship can get up, and let us help Rocinante, though he does not deserve it, for he was the main cause of all this thrashing. I never thought it of Rocinante, for I took him to be a virtuous person and as quiet as myself. After all, they say right that it takes a long time to come to know people, and that there is nothing sure in this life. Who would have said that, after such mighty slashes as your worship gave that unlucky knight-errant, there was coming, travelling post and at the very heels of them, such a great storm of sticks as has fallen upon our shoulders?"

"And yet thine, Sancho," replied Don Quixote, "ought to be used to such squalls; but mine, reared in soft cloth and fine linen, it is plain they must feel more keenly the pain of this mishap, and if it were not that I imagine—why do I say imagine?—know of a certainty that all these annoyances are very necessary accompaniments of the calling of arms, I would lay me down here to die of pure vexation."

To this the squire replied, "Senor, as these mishaps are what one reaps of chivalry, tell me if they happen very often, or if they have their own fixed times for coming to pass; because it seems to me that after two harvests we shall be no good for the third, unless God in his infinite mercy helps us."

"Know, friend Sancho," answered Don Quixote, "that the life of knights-errant is subject to a thousand dangers and reverses, and neither more nor less is it within immediate possibility for knights-errant to become kings and emperors, as experience has shown in the case of many different knights with whose histories I am thoroughly acquainted; and I could tell thee now, if the pain would let me, of some who simply by might of arm have risen to the high stations I have mentioned; and those same, both before and after, experienced divers misfortunes and miseries; for the valiant Amadis of Gaul found himself in the power of his mortal enemy Arcalaus the magician, who, it is positively asserted, holding him captive, gave him more than two hundred lashes with the reins of his horse while tied to one of the pillars of a court; and moreover there is a certain recondite author of no small authority who says that the Knight of Phoebus, being caught in a certain pitfall, which opened under his feet in a certain castle, on falling found himself bound hand and foot in a deep pit underground, where they administered to him one of those things they call clysters, of sand and snow-water, that well-nigh finished him; and if he had not been succoured in that sore extremity by a sage, a great friend of his, it would have gone very hard with the poor knight; so I may well suffer in company with such worthy folk, for greater were the indignities which they had to suffer than those which we suffer. For I would have thee know, Sancho, that wounds caused by any instruments which happen by chance to be in hand inflict no indignity, and this is laid down in the law of the duel in express words: if, for instance, the cobbler strikes another with the last which he has in his hand, though it be in fact a piece of wood, it cannot be said for that reason that he whom he struck with it has been cudgelled. I say this lest thou shouldst imagine that because we have been drubbed in this affray we have therefore suffered any indignity; for the arms those men carried, with which they pounded us, were nothing more than their stakes, and not one of them, so far as I remember, carried rapier, sword, or dagger."

"They gave me no time to see that much," answered Sancho, "for hardly had I laid hand on my tizona when they signed the cross on my shoulders with their sticks in such style that they took the sight out of my eyes and the strength out of my feet, stretching me where I now lie, and where thinking of whether all those stake-strokes were an indignity or not gives me no uneasiness, which the pain of the blows does, for they will remain as deeply impressed on my memory as on my shoulders."

"For all that let me tell thee, brother Panza," said Don Quixote, "that there is no recollection which time does not put an end to, and no pain which death does not remove."

"And what greater misfortune can there be," replied Panza, "than the one that waits for time to put an end to it and death to remove it? If our mishap were one of those that are cured with a couple of plasters, it would not be so bad; but I am beginning to think that all the plasters in a hospital almost won't be enough to put us right."

"No more of that: pluck strength out of weakness, Sancho, as I mean to do," returned Don Quixote, "and let us see how Rocinante is, for it seems to me that not the least share of this mishap has fallen to the lot of the poor beast."

"There is nothing wonderful in that," replied Sancho, "since he is a knight-errant too; what I wonder at is that my beast should have come off scot-free where we come out scotched."

"Fortune always leaves a door open in adversity in order to bring relief to it," said Don Quixote; "I say so because this little beast may now supply the want of Rocinante, carrying me hence to some castle where I may be cured of my wounds. And moreover I shall not hold it any dishonour to be so mounted, for I remember having read how the good old Silenus, the tutor and instructor of the gay god of laughter, when he entered the city of the hundred gates, went very contentedly mounted on a handsome ass."

"It may be true that he went mounted as your worship says," answered Sancho, "but there is a great difference between going mounted and going slung like a sack of manure."

To which Don Quixote replied, "Wounds received in battle confer honour instead of taking it away; and so, friend Panza, say no more, but, as I told thee before, get up as well as thou canst and put me on top of thy beast in whatever fashion pleases thee best, and let us go hence ere night come on and surprise us in these wilds."

"And yet I have heard your worship say," observed Panza, "that it is very meet for knights-errant to sleep in wastes and deserts, and that they esteem it very good fortune."

"That is," said Don Quixote, "when they cannot help it, or when they are in love; and so true is this that there have been knights who have remained two years on rocks, in sunshine and shade and all the inclemencies of heaven, without their ladies knowing anything of it; and one of these was Amadis, when, under the name of Beltenebros, he took up his abode on the Pena Pobre for—I know not if it was eight years or eight months, for I am not very sure of the reckoning; at any rate he stayed there doing penance for I know not what pique the Princess Oriana had against him; but no more of this now, Sancho, and make haste before a mishap like Rocinante's befalls the ass."

"The very devil would be in it in that case," said Sancho; and letting off thirty "ohs," and sixty sighs, and a hundred and twenty maledictions and execrations on whomsoever it was that had brought him there, he raised himself, stopping half-way bent like a Turkish bow without power to bring himself upright, but with all his pains he saddled his ass, who too had gone astray somewhat, yielding to the excessive licence of the day; he next raised up Rocinante, and as for him, had he possessed a tongue to complain with, most assuredly neither Sancho nor his master would have been behind him.

To be brief, Sancho fixed Don Quixote on the ass and secured Rocinante with a leading rein, and taking the ass by the halter, he proceeded more or less in the direction in which it seemed to him the high road might be; and, as chance was conducting their affairs for them from good to better, he had not gone a short league when the road came in sight, and on it he perceived an inn, which to his annoyance and to the delight of Don Quixote must needs be a castle. Sancho insisted that it was an inn, and his master that it was not one, but a castle, and the dispute lasted so long that before the point was settled they had time to reach it, and into it Sancho entered with all his team without any further controversy.

CHAPTER XVI.

OF WHAT HAPPENED TO THE INGENIOUS GENTLEMAN IN THE INN WHICH HE TOOK TO BE A CASTLE

The innkeeper, seeing Don Quixote slung across the ass, asked Sancho what was amiss with him. Sancho answered that it was nothing, only that he had fallen down from a rock and had his ribs a little bruised. The innkeeper had a wife whose disposition was not such as those of her calling commonly have, for she was by nature kind-hearted and felt for the sufferings of her neighbours, so she at once set about tending Don Quixote, and made her young daughter, a very comely girl, help her in taking care of her guest. There was besides in the inn, as servant, an Asturian lass with a broad face, flat poll, and snub nose, blind of one eye and not very sound in the other. The elegance of her shape, to be sure, made up for all her defects; she did not measure seven palms from head to foot, and her shoulders, which overweighted her somewhat, made her contemplate the ground more than she liked. This graceful lass, then, helped the young girl, and the two made up a very bad bed for Don Quixote in a garret that showed evident signs of having formerly served for many years as a straw-loft, in which there was also quartered a carrier whose bed was placed a little beyond our Don Quixote's, and, though only made of the pack-saddles and cloths of his mules, had much the advantage of it, as Don Quixote's consisted simply of four rough boards on two not very even trestles, a mattress, that for thinness might have passed for a quilt, full of pellets which, were they not seen through the rents to be wool, would to the touch have seemed pebbles in hardness, two sheets made of buckler leather, and a coverlet the threads of which anyone that chose might have counted without missing one in the reckoning.

On this accursed bed Don Quixote stretched himself, and the hostess and her daughter soon covered him with plasters from top to toe, while Maritornes—for that was the name of the Asturian—held the light for them, and while plastering him, the hostess, observing how full of wheals Don Quixote was in some places, remarked that this had more the look of blows than of a fall.

It was not blows, Sancho said, but that the rock had many points and projections, and that each of them had left its mark. "Pray, senora," he added, "manage to save some tow, as there will be no want of some one to use it, for my loins too are rather sore."

"Then you must have fallen too," said the hostess.

"I did not fall," said Sancho Panza, "but from the shock I got at seeing my master fall, my body aches so that I feel as if I had had a thousand thwacks."

"That may well be," said the young girl, "for it has many a time happened to me to dream that I was falling down from a tower and never coming to the ground, and when I awoke from the dream to find myself as weak and shaken as if I had really fallen."

"There is the point, senora," replied Sancho Panza, "that I without dreaming at all, but being more awake than I am now, find myself with scarcely less wheals than my master, Don Quixote."

"How is the gentleman called?" asked Maritornes the Asturian.

"Don Quixote of La Mancha," answered Sancho Panza, "and he is a knight-adventurer, and one of the best and stoutest that have been seen in the world this long time past."

"What is a knight-adventurer?" said the lass.

"Are you so new in the world as not to know?" answered Sancho Panza. "Well, then, you must know, sister, that a knight-adventurer is a thing that in two words is seen drubbed and emperor, that is to-day the most miserable and needy being in the world, and to-morrow will have two or three crowns of kingdoms to give his squire."

"Then how is it," said the hostess, "that belonging to so good a master as this, you have not, to judge by appearances, even so much as a county?"

"It is too soon yet," answered Sancho, "for we have only been a month going in quest of adventures, and so far we have met with nothing that can be called one, for it will happen that when one thing is looked for another thing is found; however, if my master Don Quixote gets well of this wound, or fall, and I am left none the worse of it, I would not change my hopes for the best title in Spain."

To all this conversation Don Quixote was listening very attentively, and sitting up in bed as well as he could, and taking the hostess by the hand he said to her, "Believe me, fair lady, you may call yourself fortunate in having in this castle of yours sheltered my person, which is such that if I do not myself praise it, it is because of what is commonly said, that self-praise debaseth; but my squire will inform you who I am. I only tell you that I shall preserve for ever inscribed on my memory the service you have rendered me in order to tender you my gratitude while life shall last me; and would to Heaven love held me not so enthralled and subject to its laws and to the eyes of that fair ingrate whom I name between my teeth, but that those of this lovely damsel might be the masters of my liberty."

The hostess, her daughter, and the worthy Maritornes listened in bewilderment to the words of the knight-errant; for they understood about as much of them as if he had been talking Greek, though they could perceive they were all meant for expressions of good-will and blandishments; and not being accustomed to this kind of language, they stared at him and wondered to themselves, for he seemed to them a man of a different sort from those they were used to, and thanking him in pothouse phrase for his civility they left him, while the Asturian gave her attention to Sancho, who needed it no less than his master.

The carrier had made an arrangement with her for recreation that night, and she had given him her word that when the guests were quiet and the family asleep she would come in search of him and meet his wishes unreservedly. And it is said of this good lass that she never made promises of the kind without fulfilling them, even though she made them in a forest and without any witness present, for she plumed herself greatly on being a lady and held it no disgrace to be in such an employment as servant in an inn, because, she said, misfortunes and ill-luck had brought her to that position. The hard, narrow, wretched, rickety bed of Don Quixote stood first in the middle of this star-lit stable, and close beside it Sancho made his, which merely consisted of a rush mat and a blanket that looked as if it was of threadbare canvas rather than of wool. Next to these two beds was that of the carrier, made up, as has been said, of the pack-saddles and all the trappings of the two best mules he had, though there were twelve of them, sleek, plump, and in prime condition, for he was one of the rich carriers of Arevalo, according to the author of this history, who particularly mentions this carrier because he knew him very well, and they even say was in some degree a relation of his; besides which Cide Hamete Benengeli was a historian of great research and accuracy in all things, as is very evident since he would not pass over in silence those that have been already mentioned, however trifling and insignificant they might be, an example that might be followed by those grave historians who relate transactions so curtly and briefly that we hardly get a taste of them, all the substance of the work being left in the inkstand from carelessness, perverseness, or ignorance. A thousand blessings on the author of "Tablante de Ricamonte" and that of the other book in which the deeds of the Conde Tomillas are recounted; with what minuteness they describe everything!

To proceed, then: after having paid a visit to his team and given them their second feed, the carrier stretched himself on his pack-saddles and lay waiting for his conscientious Maritornes. Sancho was by this time plastered and had lain down, and though he strove to sleep the pain of his ribs would not let him, while Don Quixote with the pain of his had his eyes as wide open as a hare's.

The inn was all in silence, and in the whole of it there was no light except that given by a lantern that hung burning in the middle of the gateway. This strange stillness, and the thoughts, always present to our knight's mind, of the incidents described at every turn in the books that were the cause of his misfortune, conjured up to his imagination as extraordinary a delusion as can well be conceived, which was that he fancied himself to have reached a famous castle (for, as has been said, all the inns he lodged in were castles to his eyes), and that the daughter of the innkeeper was daughter of the lord of the castle, and that she, won by his high-bred bearing, had fallen in love with him, and had promised to come to his bed for a while that night without the knowledge of her parents; and holding all this fantasy that he had constructed as solid fact, he began to feel uneasy and to consider the perilous risk which his virtue was about to encounter, and he resolved in his heart to commit no treason to his lady Dulcinea del Toboso, even though the queen Guinevere herself and the dame Quintanona should present themselves before him.

While he was taken up with these vagaries, then, the time and the hour—an unlucky one for him—arrived for the Asturian to come, who in her smock, with bare feet and her hair gathered into a fustian coif, with noiseless and cautious steps entered the chamber where the three were quartered, in quest of the carrier; but scarcely had she gained the door when Don Quixote perceived her, and sitting up in his bed in spite of his plasters and the pain of his ribs, he stretched out his arms to receive his beauteous damsel. The Asturian, who went all doubled up and in silence with her hands before her feeling for her lover, encountered the arms of Don Quixote, who grasped her tightly by the wrist, and drawing her towards him, while she dared not utter a word, made her sit down on the bed. He then felt her smock, and although it was of sackcloth it appeared to him to be of the finest and softest silk: on her wrists she wore some glass beads, but to him they had the sheen of precious Orient pearls: her hair, which in some measure resembled a horse's mane, he rated as threads of the brightest gold of Araby, whose refulgence dimmed the sun himself: her breath, which no doubt smelt of yesterday's stale salad, seemed to him to diffuse a sweet aromatic fragrance from her mouth; and, in short, he drew her portrait in his imagination with the same features and in the same style as that which he had seen in his books of the other princesses who, smitten by love, came with all the adornments that are here set down, to see the sorely wounded knight; and so great was the poor gentleman's blindness that neither touch, nor smell, nor anything else about the good lass that would have made any but a carrier vomit, were enough to undeceive him; on the contrary, he was persuaded he had the goddess of beauty in his arms, and holding her firmly in his grasp he went on to say in low, tender voice:

"Would that found myself, lovely and exalted lady, in a position to repay such a favour as that which you, by the sight of your great beauty, have granted me; but fortune, which is never weary of persecuting the good, has chosen to place me upon this bed, where I lie so bruised and broken that though my inclination would gladly comply with yours it is impossible; besides, to this impossibility another yet greater is to be added, which is the faith that I have pledged to the peerless Dulcinea del Toboso, sole lady of my most secret thoughts; and were it not that this stood in the way I should not be so insensible a knight as to miss the happy opportunity which your great goodness has offered me."

Maritornes was fretting and sweating at finding herself held so fast by Don Quixote, and not understanding or heeding the words he addressed to her, she strove without speaking to free herself. The worthy carrier, whose unholy thoughts kept him awake, was aware of his doxy the moment she entered the door, and was listening attentively to all Don Quixote said; and jealous that the Asturian should have broken her word with him for another, drew nearer to Don Quixote's bed and stood still to see what would come of this talk which he could not understand; but when he perceived the wench struggling to get free and Don Quixote striving to hold her, not relishing the joke he raised his arm and delivered such a terrible cuff on the lank jaws of the amorous knight that he bathed all his mouth in blood, and not content with this he mounted on his ribs and with his feet tramped all over them at a pace rather smarter than a trot. The bed which was somewhat crazy and not very firm on its feet, unable to support the additional weight of the carrier, came to the ground, and at the mighty crash of this the innkeeper awoke and at once concluded that it must be some brawl of Maritornes', because after calling loudly to her he got no answer. With this suspicion he got up, and lighting a lamp hastened to the quarter where he had heard the disturbance. The wench, seeing that her master was coming and knowing that his temper was terrible, frightened and panic-stricken made for the bed of Sancho Panza, who still slept, and crouching upon it made a ball of herself.

The innkeeper came in exclaiming, "Where art thou, strumpet? Of course this is some of thy work." At this Sancho awoke, and feeling this mass almost on top of him fancied he had the nightmare and began to distribute fisticuffs all round, of which a certain share fell upon Maritornes, who, irritated by the pain and flinging modesty aside, paid back so many in return to Sancho that she woke him up in spite of himself. He then, finding himself so handled, by whom he knew not, raising himself up as well as he could, grappled with Maritornes, and he and she between them began the bitterest and drollest scrimmage in the world. The carrier, however, perceiving by the light of the innkeeper candle how it fared with his ladylove, quitting Don Quixote, ran to bring her the help she needed; and the innkeeper did the same but with a different intention, for his was to chastise the lass, as he believed that beyond a doubt she alone was the cause of all the harmony. And so, as the saying is, cat to rat, rat to rope, rope to stick, the carrier pounded Sancho, Sancho the lass, she him, and the innkeeper her, and all worked away so briskly that they did not give themselves a moment's rest; and the best of it was that the innkeeper's lamp went out, and as they were left in the dark they all laid on one upon the other in a mass so unmercifully that there was not a sound spot left where a hand could light.

It so happened that there was lodging that night in the inn a caudrillero of what they call the Old Holy Brotherhood of Toledo, who, also hearing the extraordinary noise of the conflict, seized his staff and the tin case with his warrants, and made his way in the dark into the room crying: "Hold! in the name of the Jurisdiction! Hold! in the name of the Holy Brotherhood!"

The first that he came upon was the pummelled Don Quixote, who lay stretched senseless on his back upon his broken-down bed, and, his hand falling on the beard as he felt about, he continued to cry, "Help for the Jurisdiction!" but perceiving that he whom he had laid hold of did not move or stir, he concluded that he was dead and that those in the room were his murderers, and with this suspicion he raised his voice still higher, calling out, "Shut the inn gate; see that no one goes out; they have killed a man here!" This cry startled them all, and each dropped the contest at the point at which the voice reached him. The innkeeper retreated to his room, the carrier to his pack-saddles, the lass to her crib; the unlucky Don Quixote and Sancho alone were unable to move from where they were. The cuadrillero on this let go Don Quixote's beard, and went out to look for a light to search for and apprehend the culprits; but not finding one, as the innkeeper had purposely extinguished the lantern on retreating to his room, he was compelled to have recourse to the hearth, where after much time and trouble he lit another lamp.

CHAPTER XVII.

IN WHICH ARE CONTAINED THE INNUMERABLE TROUBLES WHICH THE BRAVE DON QUIXOTE AND HIS GOOD SQUIRE SANCHO PANZA ENDURED IN THE INN, WHICH TO HIS MISFORTUNE HE TOOK TO BE A CASTLE

By this time Don Quixote had recovered from his swoon; and in the same tone of voice in which he had called to his squire the day before when he lay stretched "in the vale of the stakes," he began calling to him now, "Sancho, my friend, art thou asleep? sleepest thou, friend Sancho?"

"How can I sleep, curses on it!" returned Sancho discontentedly and bitterly, "when it is plain that all the devils have been at me this night?"

"Thou mayest well believe that," answered Don Quixote, "because, either I know little, or this castle is enchanted, for thou must know-but this that I am now about to tell thee thou must swear to keep secret until after my death."

"I swear it," answered Sancho.

"I say so," continued Don Quixote, "because I hate taking away anyone's good name."

"I say," replied Sancho, "that I swear to hold my tongue about it till the end of your worship's days, and God grant I may be able to let it out tomorrow."

"Do I do thee such injuries, Sancho," said Don Quixote, "that thou wouldst see me dead so soon?"

"It is not for that," replied Sancho, "but because I hate keeping things long, and I don't want them to grow rotten with me from over-keeping."

"At any rate," said Don Quixote, "I have more confidence in thy affection and good nature; and so I would have thee know that this night there befell me one of the strangest adventures that I could describe, and to relate it to thee briefly thou must know that a little while ago the daughter of the lord of this castle came to me, and that she is the most elegant and beautiful damsel that could be found in the wide world. What I could tell thee of the charms of her person! of her lively wit! of other secret matters which, to preserve the fealty I owe to my lady Dulcinea del Toboso, I shall pass over unnoticed and in silence! I will only tell thee that, either fate being envious of so great a boon placed in my hands by good fortune, or perhaps (and this is more probable) this castle being, as I have already said, enchanted, at the time when I was engaged in the sweetest and most amorous discourse with her, there came, without my seeing or knowing whence it came, a hand attached to some arm of some huge giant, that planted such a cuff on my jaws that I have them all bathed in blood, and then pummelled me in such a way that I am in a worse plight than yesterday when the carriers, on account of Rocinante's misbehaviour, inflicted on us the injury thou knowest of; whence conjecture that there must be some enchanted Moor guarding the treasure of this damsel's beauty, and that it is not for me."

"Not for me either," said Sancho, "for more than four hundred Moors have so thrashed me that the drubbing of the stakes was cakes and fancy-bread to it. But tell me, senor, what do you call this excellent and rare adventure that has left us as we are left now? Though your worship was not so badly off, having in your arms that incomparable beauty you spoke of; but I, what did I have, except the heaviest whacks I think I had in all my life? Unlucky me and the mother that bore me! for I am not a knight-errant and never expect to be one, and of all the mishaps, the greater part falls to my share."

"Then thou hast been thrashed too?" said Don Quixote.

"Didn't I say so? worse luck to my line!" said Sancho.

"Be not distressed, friend," said Don Quixote, "for I will now make the precious balsam with which we shall cure ourselves in the twinkling of an eye."

By this time the cuadrillero had succeeded in lighting the lamp, and came in to see the man that he thought had been killed; and as Sancho caught sight of him at the door, seeing him coming in his shirt, with a cloth on his head, and a lamp in his hand, and a very forbidding countenance, he said to his master, "Senor, can it be that this is the enchanted Moor coming back to give us more castigation if there be anything still left in the ink-bottle?"

"It cannot be the Moor," answered Don Quixote, "for those under enchantment do not let themselves be seen by anyone."

"If they don't let themselves be seen, they let themselves be felt," said

Sancho; "if not, let my shoulders speak to the point."

"Mine could speak too," said Don Quixote, "but that is not a sufficient reason for believing that what we see is the enchanted Moor."

The officer came up, and finding them engaged in such a peaceful conversation, stood amazed; though Don Quixote, to be sure, still lay on his back unable to move from pure pummelling and plasters. The officer turned to him and said, "Well, how goes it, good man?"

"I would speak more politely if I were you," replied Don Quixote; "is it the way of this country to address knights-errant in that style, you booby?"

The cuadrillero finding himself so disrespectfully treated by such a sorry-looking individual, lost his temper, and raising the lamp full of oil, smote Don Quixote such a blow with it on the head that he gave him a badly broken pate; then, all being in darkness, he went out, and Sancho Panza said, "That is certainly the enchanted Moor, Senor, and he keeps the treasure for others, and for us only the cuffs and lamp-whacks."

"That is the truth," answered Don Quixote, "and there is no use in troubling oneself about these matters of enchantment or being angry or vexed at them, for as they are invisible and visionary we shall find no one on whom to avenge ourselves, do what we may; rise, Sancho, if thou canst, and call the alcaide of this fortress, and get him to give me a little oil, wine, salt, and rosemary to make the salutiferous balsam, for indeed I believe I have great need of it now, because I am losing much blood from the wound that phantom gave me."

Sancho got up with pain enough in his bones, and went after the innkeeper in the dark, and meeting the officer, who was looking to see what had become of his enemy, he said to him, "Senor, whoever you are, do us the favour and kindness to give us a little rosemary, oil, salt, and wine, for it is wanted to cure one of the best knights-errant on earth, who lies on yonder bed wounded by the hands of the enchanted Moor that is in this inn."

When the officer heard him talk in this way, he took him for a man out of his senses, and as day was now beginning to break, he opened the inn gate, and calling the host, he told him what this good man wanted. The host furnished him with what he required, and Sancho brought it to Don Quixote, who, with his hand to his head, was bewailing the pain of the blow of the lamp, which had done him no more harm than raising a couple of rather large lumps, and what he fancied blood was only the sweat that flowed from him in his sufferings during the late storm. To be brief, he took the materials, of which he made a compound, mixing them all and boiling them a good while until it seemed to him they had come to perfection. He then asked for some vial to pour it into, and as there was not one in the inn, he decided on putting it into a tin oil-bottle or flask of which the host made him a free gift; and over the flask he repeated more than eighty paternosters and as many more ave-marias, salves, and credos, accompanying each word with a cross by way of benediction, at all which there were present Sancho, the innkeeper, and the cuadrillero; for the carrier was now peacefully engaged in attending to the comfort of his mules.

This being accomplished, he felt anxious to make trial himself, on the spot, of the virtue of this precious balsam, as he considered it, and so he drank near a quart of what could not be put into the flask and remained in the pigskin in which it had been boiled; but scarcely had he done drinking when he began to vomit in such a way that nothing was left in his stomach, and with the pangs and spasms of vomiting he broke into a profuse sweat, on account of which he bade them cover him up and leave him alone. They did so, and he lay sleeping more than three hours, at the end of which he awoke and felt very great bodily relief and so much ease from his bruises that he thought himself quite cured, and verily believed he had hit upon the balsam of Fierabras; and that with this remedy he might thenceforward, without any fear, face any kind of destruction, battle, or combat, however perilous it might be.

Sancho Panza, who also regarded the amendment of his master as miraculous, begged him to give him what was left in the pigskin, which was no small quantity. Don Quixote consented, and he, taking it with both hands, in good faith and with a better will, gulped down and drained off very little less than his master. But the fact is, that the stomach of poor Sancho was of necessity not so delicate as that of his master, and so, before vomiting, he was seized with such gripings and retchings, and such sweats and faintness, that verily and truly he believed his last hour had come, and finding himself so racked and tormented he cursed the balsam and the thief that had given it to him.

Don Quixote seeing him in this state said, "It is my belief, Sancho, that this mischief comes of thy not being dubbed a knight, for I am persuaded this liquor cannot be good for those who are not so."

"If your worship knew that," returned Sancho—"woe betide me and all my kindred!—why did you let me taste it?"

At this moment the draught took effect, and the poor squire began to discharge both ways at such a rate that the rush mat on which he had thrown himself and the canvas blanket he had covering him were fit for nothing afterwards. He sweated and perspired with such paroxysms and convulsions that not only he himself but all present thought his end had come. This tempest and tribulation lasted about two hours, at the end of which he was left, not like his master, but so weak and exhausted that he could not stand. Don Quixote, however, who, as has been said, felt himself relieved and well, was eager to take his departure at once in quest of adventures, as it seemed to him that all the time he loitered there was a fraud upon the world and those in it who stood in need of his help and protection, all the more when he had the security and confidence his balsam afforded him; and so, urged by this impulse, he saddled Rocinante himself and put the pack-saddle on his squire's beast, whom likewise he helped to dress and mount the ass; after which he mounted his horse and turning to a corner of the inn he laid hold of a pike that stood there, to serve him by way of a lance. All that were in the inn, who were more than twenty persons, stood watching him; the innkeeper's daughter was likewise observing him, and he too never took his eyes off her, and from time to time fetched a sigh that he seemed to pluck up from the depths of his bowels; but they all thought it must be from the pain he felt in his ribs; at any rate they who had seen him plastered the night before thought so.

As soon as they were both mounted, at the gate of the inn, he called to the host and said in a very grave and measured voice, "Many and great are the favours, Senor Alcaide, that I have received in this castle of yours, and I remain under the deepest obligation to be grateful to you for them all the days of my life; if I can repay them in avenging you of any arrogant foe who may have wronged you, know that my calling is no other than to aid the weak, to avenge those who suffer wrong, and to chastise perfidy. Search your memory, and if you find anything of this kind you need only tell me of it, and I promise you by the order of knighthood which I have received to procure you satisfaction and reparation to the utmost of your desire."

The innkeeper replied to him with equal calmness, "Sir Knight, I do not want your worship to avenge me of any wrong, because when any is done me I can take what vengeance seems good to me; the only thing I want is that you pay me the score that you have run up in the inn last night, as well for the straw and barley for your two beasts, as for supper and beds."

"Then this is an inn?" said Don Quixote.

"And a very respectable one," said the innkeeper.

"I have been under a mistake all this time," answered Don Quixote, "for in truth I thought it was a castle, and not a bad one; but since it appears that it is not a castle but an inn, all that can be done now is that you should excuse the payment, for I cannot contravene the rule of knights-errant, of whom I know as a fact (and up to the present I have read nothing to the contrary) that they never paid for lodging or anything else in the inn where they might be; for any hospitality that might be offered them is their due by law and right in return for the insufferable toil they endure in seeking adventures by night and by day, in summer and in winter, on foot and on horseback, in hunger and thirst, cold and heat, exposed to all the inclemencies of heaven and all the hardships of earth."

"I have little to do with that," replied the innkeeper; "pay me what you owe me, and let us have no more talk of chivalry, for all I care about is to get my money."

"You are a stupid, scurvy innkeeper," said Don Quixote, and putting spurs to Rocinante and bringing his pike to the slope he rode out of the inn before anyone could stop him, and pushed on some distance without looking to see if his squire was following him.

The innkeeper when he saw him go without paying him ran to get payment of Sancho, who said that as his master would not pay neither would he, because, being as he was squire to a knight-errant, the same rule and reason held good for him as for his master with regard to not paying anything in inns and hostelries. At this the innkeeper waxed very wroth, and threatened if he did not pay to compel him in a way that he would not like. To which Sancho made answer that by the law of chivalry his master had received he would not pay a rap, though it cost him his life; for the excellent and ancient usage of knights-errant was not going to be violated by him, nor should the squires of such as were yet to come into the world ever complain of him or reproach him with breaking so just a privilege.

The ill-luck of the unfortunate Sancho so ordered it that among the company in the inn there were four woolcarders from Segovia, three needle-makers from the Colt of Cordova, and two lodgers from the Fair of Seville, lively fellows, tender-hearted, fond of a joke, and playful, who, almost as if instigated and moved by a common impulse, made up to Sancho and dismounted him from his ass, while one of them went in for the blanket of the host's bed; but on flinging him into it they looked up, and seeing that the ceiling was somewhat lower than what they required for their work, they decided upon going out into the yard, which was bounded by the sky, and there, putting Sancho in the middle of the blanket, they began to raise him high, making sport with him as they would with a dog at Shrovetide.

The cries of the poor blanketed wretch were so loud that they reached the ears of his master, who, halting to listen attentively, was persuaded that some new adventure was coming, until he clearly perceived that it was his squire who uttered them. Wheeling about he came up to the inn with a laborious gallop, and finding it shut went round it to see if he could find some way of getting in; but as soon as he came to the wall of the yard, which was not very high, he discovered the game that was being played with his squire. He saw him rising and falling in the air with such grace and nimbleness that, had his rage allowed him, it is my belief he would have laughed. He tried to climb from his horse on to the top of the wall, but he was so bruised and battered that he could not even dismount; and so from the back of his horse he began to utter such maledictions and objurgations against those who were blanketing Sancho as it would be impossible to write down accurately: they, however, did not stay their laughter or their work for this, nor did the flying Sancho cease his lamentations, mingled now with threats, now with entreaties but all to little purpose, or none at all, until from pure weariness they left off. They then brought him his ass, and mounting him on top of it they put his jacket round him; and the compassionate Maritornes, seeing him so exhausted, thought fit to refresh him with a jug of water, and that it might be all the cooler she fetched it from the well. Sancho took it, and as he was raising it to his mouth he was stopped by the cries of his master exclaiming, "Sancho, my son, drink not water; drink it not, my son, for it will kill thee; see, here I have the blessed balsam (and he held up the flask of liquor), and with drinking two drops of it thou wilt certainly be restored."

At these words Sancho turned his eyes asquint, and in a still louder voice said, "Can it be your worship has forgotten that I am not a knight, or do you want me to end by vomiting up what bowels I have left after last night? Keep your liquor in the name of all the devils, and leave me to myself!" and at one and the same instant he left off talking and began drinking; but as at the first sup he perceived it was water he did not care to go on with it, and begged Maritornes to fetch him some wine, which she did with right good will, and paid for it with her own money; for indeed they say of her that, though she was in that line of life, there was some faint and distant resemblance to a Christian about her. When Sancho had done drinking he dug his heels into his ass, and the gate of the inn being thrown open he passed out very well pleased at having paid nothing and carried his point, though it had been at the expense of his usual sureties, his shoulders. It is true that the innkeeper detained his alforjas in payment of what was owing to him, but Sancho took his departure in such a flurry that he never missed them. The innkeeper, as soon as he saw him off, wanted to bar the gate close, but the blanketers would not agree to it, for they were fellows who would not have cared two farthings for Don Quixote, even had he been really one of the knights-errant of the Round Table.

CHAPTER XVIII.

IN WHICH IS RELATED THE DISCOURSE SANCHO PANZA HELD WITH HIS MASTER, DON QUIXOTE, AND OTHER ADVENTURES WORTH RELATING

Sancho reached his master so limp and faint that he could not urge on his beast. When Don Quixote saw the state he was in he said, "I have now come to the conclusion, good Sancho, that this castle or inn is beyond a doubt enchanted, because those who have so atrociously diverted themselves with thee, what can they be but phantoms or beings of another world? and I hold this confirmed by having noticed that when I was by the wall of the yard witnessing the acts of thy sad tragedy, it was out of my power to mount upon it, nor could I even dismount from Rocinante, because they no doubt had me enchanted;

for I swear to thee by the faith of what I am that if I had been able to climb up or dismount, I would have avenged thee in such a way that those braggart thieves would have remembered their freak for ever, even though in so doing I knew that I contravened the laws of chivalry, which, as I have often told thee, do not permit a knight to lay hands on him who is not one, save in case of urgent and great necessity in defence of his own life and person."

"I would have avenged myself too if I could," said Sancho, "whether I had been dubbed knight or not, but I could not; though for my part I am persuaded those who amused themselves with me were not phantoms or enchanted men, as your worship says, but men of flesh and bone like ourselves; and they all had their names, for I heard them name them when they were tossing me, and one was called Pedro Martinez, and another Tenorio Hernandez, and the innkeeper, I heard, was called Juan Palomeque the Left-handed; so that, senor, your not being able to leap over the wall of the yard or dismount from your horse came of something else besides enchantments; and what I make out clearly from all this is, that these adventures we go seeking will in the end lead us into such misadventures that we shall not know which is our right foot; and that the best and wisest thing, according to my small wits, would be for us to return home, now that it is harvest-time, and attend to our business, and give over wandering from Zeca to Mecca and from pail to bucket, as the saying is."

"How little thou knowest about chivalry, Sancho," replied Don Quixote; "hold thy peace and have patience; the day will come when thou shalt see with thine own eyes what an honourable thing it is to wander in the pursuit of this calling; nay, tell me, what greater pleasure can there be in the world, or what delight can equal that of winning a battle, and triumphing over one's enemy? None, beyond all doubt."

"Very likely," answered Sancho, "though I do not know it; all I know is that since we have been knights-errant, or since your worship has been one (for I have no right to reckon myself one of so honourable a number) we have never won any battle except the one with the Biscayan, and even out of that your worship came with half an ear and half a helmet the less; and from that till now it has been all cudgellings and more cudgellings, cuffs and more cuffs, I getting the blanketing over and above, and falling in with enchanted persons on whom I cannot avenge myself so as to know what the delight, as your worship calls it, of conquering an enemy is like."

"That is what vexes me, and what ought to vex thee, Sancho," replied Don Quixote; "but henceforward I will endeavour to have at hand some sword made by such craft that no kind of enchantments can take effect upon him who carries it, and it is even possible that fortune may procure for me that which belonged to Amadis when he was called 'The Knight of the Burning Sword,' which was one of the best swords that ever knight in the world possessed, for, besides having the said virtue, it cut like a razor, and there was no armour, however strong and enchanted it might be, that could resist it."

"Such is my luck," said Sancho, "that even if that happened and your worship found some such sword, it would, like the balsam, turn out serviceable and good for dubbed knights only, and as for the squires, they might sup sorrow."

"Fear not that, Sancho," said Don Quixote: "Heaven will deal better by thee."

Thus talking, Don Quixote and his squire were going along, when, on the road they were following, Don Quixote perceived approaching them a large and thick cloud of dust, on seeing which he turned to Sancho and said:

"This is the day, Sancho, on which will be seen the boon my fortune is reserving for me; this, I say, is the day on which as much as on any other shall be displayed the might of my arm, and on which I shall do deeds that shall remain written in the book of fame for all ages to come. Seest thou that cloud of dust which rises yonder? Well, then, all that is churned up by a vast army composed of various and countless nations that comes marching there."

"According to that there must be two," said Sancho, "for on this opposite side also there rises just such another cloud of dust."

Don Quixote turned to look and found that it was true, and rejoicing exceedingly, he concluded that they were two armies about to engage and encounter in the midst of that broad plain; for at all times and seasons his fancy was full of the battles, enchantments, adventures, crazy feats, loves, and defiances that are recorded in the books of chivalry, and everything he said, thought, or did had reference to such things. Now the cloud of dust he had seen was raised by two great droves of sheep coming along the same road in opposite directions, which, because of the dust, did not become visible until they drew near, but Don Quixote asserted so positively that they were armies that Sancho was led to believe it and say, "Well, and what are we to do, senor?"

"What?" said Don Quixote: "give aid and assistance to the weak and those who need it; and thou must know, Sancho, that this which comes opposite to us is conducted and led by the mighty emperor Alifanfaron, lord of the great isle of Trapobana; this other that marches behind me is that of his enemy the king of the Garamantas, Pentapolin of the Bare Arm, for he always goes into battle with his right arm bare."

"But why are these two lords such enemies?"

"They are at enmity," replied Don Quixote, "because this Alifanfaron is a furious pagan and is in love with the daughter of Pentapolin, who is a very beautiful and moreover gracious lady, and a Christian, and her father is unwilling to bestow her upon the pagan king unless he first abandons the religion of his false prophet Mahomet, and adopts his own."

"By my beard," said Sancho, "but Pentapolin does quite right, and I will help him as much as I can."

"In that thou wilt do what is thy duty, Sancho," said Don Quixote; "for to engage in battles of this sort it is not requisite to be a dubbed knight."

"That I can well understand," answered Sancho; "but where shall we put this ass where we may be sure to find him after the fray is over? for I believe it has not been the custom so far to go into battle on a beast of this kind."

"That is true," said Don Quixote, "and what you had best do with him is to leave him to take his chance whether he be lost or not, for the horses we shall have when we come out victors will be so many that even Rocinante will run a risk of being changed for another. But attend to me and observe, for I wish to give thee some account of the chief knights who accompany these two armies; and that thou mayest the better see and mark, let us withdraw to that hillock which rises yonder, whence both armies may be seen."

They did so, and placed themselves on a rising ground from which the two droves that Don Quixote made armies of might have been plainly seen if the clouds of dust they raised had not obscured them and blinded the sight; nevertheless, seeing in his imagination what he did not see and what did not exist, he began thus in a loud voice:

"That knight whom thou seest yonder in yellow armour, who bears upon his shield a lion crowned crouching at the feet of a damsel, is the valiant Laurcalco, lord of the Silver Bridge; that one in armour with flowers of gold, who bears on his shield three crowns argent on an azure field, is the dreaded Micocolembo, grand duke of Quirocia; that other of gigantic frame, on his right hand, is the ever dauntless Brandabarbaran de Boliche, lord of the three Arabias, who for armour wears that serpent skin, and has for shield a gate which, according to tradition, is one of those of the temple that Samson brought to the ground when by his death he revenged himself upon his enemies. But turn thine eyes to the other side, and thou shalt see in front and in the van of this other army the ever victorious and never vanquished Timonel of Carcajona, prince of New Biscay, who comes in armour with arms quartered azure, vert, white, and yellow, and bears on his shield a cat or on a field tawny with a motto which says Miau, which is the beginning of the name of his lady, who according to report is the peerless Miaulina, daughter of the duke Alfeniquen of the Algarve; the other, who burdens and presses the loins of that powerful charger and bears arms white as snow and a shield blank and without any device, is a novice knight, a Frenchman by birth, Pierres Papin by name, lord of the baronies of Utrique; that other, who with iron-shod heels strikes the flanks of that nimble parti-coloured zebra, and for arms bears azure vair, is the mighty duke of Nerbia, Espartafilardo del Bosque, who bears for device on his shield an asparagus plant with a motto in Castilian that says, Rastrea mi suerte." And so he went on naming a number of knights of one squadron or the other out of his imagination, and to all he assigned off-hand their arms, colours, devices, and mottoes, carried away by the illusions of his unheard-of craze; and without a pause, he continued, "People of divers nations compose this squadron in front; here are those that drink of the sweet waters of the famous Xanthus, those that scour the woody Massilian plains, those that sift the pure fine gold of Arabia Felix, those that enjoy the famed cool banks of the crystal Thermodon, those that in many and various ways divert the streams of the golden Pactolus, the Numidians, faithless in their promises, the Persians renowned in archery, the Parthians and the Medes that fight as they fly, the Arabs that ever shift their dwellings, the Scythians as cruel as they are fair, the Ethiopians with pierced lips, and an infinity of other nations whose features I recognise and descry, though I cannot recall their names. In this other squadron there come those that drink of the crystal streams of the olive-bearing Betis, those that make smooth their countenances with the water of the ever rich and golden Tagus, those that rejoice in the fertilising flow of the divine Genil, those that roam the Tartesian plains abounding in pasture, those that take their pleasure in the Elysian meadows of Jerez, the rich Manchegans crowned with ruddy ears of corn, the wearers of iron, old relics of the Gothic race, those that bathe in the Pisuerga renowned for its gentle current, those that feed their herds along the spreading pastures of the winding Guadiana famed for its hidden course, those that tremble with the cold of the pineclad Pyrenees or the dazzling snows of the lofty Apennine; in a word, as many as all Europe includes and contains."

Good God! what a number of countries and nations he named! giving to each its proper attributes with marvellous readiness; brimful and saturated with what he had read in his lying books! Sancho Panza hung upon his words without speaking, and from time to time turned to try if he could see the knights and giants his master was describing, and as he could not make out one of them he said to him:

"Senor, devil take it if there's a sign of any man you talk of, knight or giant, in the whole thing; maybe it's all enchantment, like the phantoms last night."

"How canst thou say that!" answered Don Quixote; "dost thou not hear the neighing of the steeds, the braying of the trumpets, the roll of the drums?"

"I hear nothing but a great bleating of ewes and sheep," said Sancho; which was true, for by this time the two flocks had come close.

"The fear thou art in, Sancho," said Don Quixote, "prevents thee from seeing or hearing correctly, for one of the effects of fear is to derange the senses and make things appear different from what they are; if thou art in such fear, withdraw to one side and leave me to myself, for alone I suffice to bring victory to that side to which I shall give my aid;" and so saying he gave Rocinante the spur, and putting the lance in rest, shot down the slope like a thunderbolt. Sancho shouted after him, crying, "Come back, Senor Don Quixote; I vow to God they are sheep and ewes you are charging! Come back! Unlucky the father that begot me! what madness is this! Look, there is no giant, nor knight, nor cats, nor arms, nor shields quartered or whole, nor vair azure or bedevilled. What are you about? Sinner that I am before God!" But not for all these entreaties did Don Quixote turn back; on the contrary he went on shouting out, "Ho, knights, ye who follow and fight under the banners of the valiant emperor Pentapolin of the Bare Arm, follow me all; ye shall see how easily I shall give him his revenge over his enemy Alifanfaron of the Trapobana."

So saying, he dashed into the midst of the squadron of ewes, and began spearing them with as much spirit and intrepidity as if he were transfixing mortal enemies in earnest. The shepherds and drovers accompanying the flock shouted to him to desist; seeing it was no use, they ungirt their slings and began to salute his ears with stones as big as one's fist. Don Quixote gave no heed to the stones, but, letting drive right and left kept saying:

"Where art thou, proud Alifanfaron? Come before me; I am a single knight who would fain prove thy prowess hand to hand, and make thee yield thy life a penalty for the wrong thou dost to the valiant Pentapolin Garamanta." Here came a sugar-plum from the brook that struck him on the side and buried a couple of ribs in his body. Feeling himself so smitten, he imagined himself slain or badly wounded for certain, and recollecting his liquor he drew out his flask, and putting it to his mouth began to pour the contents into his stomach; but ere he had succeeded in swallowing what seemed to him enough, there came another almond which struck him on the hand and on the flask so fairly that it smashed it to pieces, knocking three or four teeth and grinders out of his mouth in its course, and sorely crushing two fingers of his hand. Such was the force of the first blow and of the second, that the poor knight in spite of himself came down backwards off his horse. The shepherds came up, and felt sure they had killed him; so in all haste they collected their flock together, took up the dead beasts, of which there were more than seven, and made off without waiting to ascertain anything further.

All this time Sancho stood on the hill watching the crazy feats his master was performing, and tearing his beard and cursing the hour and the occasion when fortune had made him acquainted with him. Seeing him, then, brought to the ground, and that the shepherds had taken themselves off, he ran to him and found him in very bad case, though not unconscious; and said he:

"Did I not tell you to come back, Senor Don Quixote; and that what you were going to attack were not armies but droves of sheep?"

"That's how that thief of a sage, my enemy, can alter and falsify things," answered Don Quixote; "thou must know, Sancho, that it is a very easy matter for those of his sort to make us believe what they choose; and this malignant being who persecutes me, envious of the glory he knew I was to win in this battle, has turned the squadrons of the enemy into droves of sheep. At any rate, do this much, I beg of thee, Sancho, to undeceive thyself, and see that what I say is true; mount thy ass and follow them quietly, and thou shalt see that when they have gone some little distance from this they will return to their original shape and, ceasing to be sheep, become men in all respects as I described them to thee at first. But go not just yet, for I want thy help and assistance; come hither, and see how many of my teeth and grinders are missing, for I feel as if there was not one left in my mouth."

Sancho came so close that he almost put his eyes into his mouth; now just at that moment the balsam had acted on the stomach of Don Quixote, so, at the very instant when Sancho came to examine his mouth, he discharged all its contents with more force than a musket, and full into the beard of the compassionate squire.

"Holy Mary!" cried Sancho, "what is this that has happened me? Clearly this sinner is mortally wounded, as he vomits blood from the mouth;" but considering the matter a little more closely he perceived by the colour, taste, and smell, that it was not blood but the balsam from the flask which he had seen him drink; and he was taken with such a loathing that his stomach turned, and he vomited up his inside over his very master, and both were left in a precious state. Sancho ran to his ass to get something wherewith to clean himself, and relieve his master, out of his alforjas; but not finding them, he well-nigh took leave of his senses, and cursed himself anew, and in his heart resolved to quit his master and return home, even though he forfeited the wages of his service and all hopes of the promised island.

Don Quixote now rose, and putting his left hand to his mouth to keep his teeth from falling out altogether, with the other he laid hold of the bridle of Rocinante, who had never stirred from his master's side—so loyal and well-behaved was he—and betook himself to where the squire stood leaning over his ass with his hand to his cheek, like one in deep dejection. Seeing him in this mood, looking so sad, Don Quixote said to him:

"Bear in mind, Sancho, that one man is no more than another, unless he does more than another; all these tempests that fall upon us are signs that fair weather is coming shortly, and that things will go well with us, for it is impossible for good or evil to last for ever; and hence it follows that the evil having lasted long, the good must be now nigh at hand; so thou must not distress thyself at the misfortunes which happen to me, since thou hast no share in them."

"How have I not?" replied Sancho; "was he whom they blanketed yesterday perchance any other than my father's son? and the alforjas that are missing to-day with all my treasures, did they belong to any other but myself?"

"What! are the alforjas missing, Sancho?" said Don Quixote.

"Yes, they are missing," answered Sancho.

"In that case we have nothing to eat to-day," replied Don Quixote.

"It would be so," answered Sancho, "if there were none of the herbs your worship says you know in these meadows, those with which knights-errant as unlucky as your worship are wont to supply such-like shortcomings."

"For all that," answered Don Quixote, "I would rather have just now a quarter of bread, or a loaf and a couple of pilchards' heads, than all the herbs described by Dioscorides, even with Doctor Laguna's notes. Nevertheless, Sancho the Good, mount thy beast and come along with me, for God, who provides for all things, will not fail us (more especially when we are so active in his service as we are), since he fails not the midges of the air, nor the grubs of the earth, nor the tadpoles of the water, and is so merciful that he maketh his sun to rise on the good and on the evil, and sendeth rain on the unjust and on the just."

"Your worship would make a better preacher than knight-errant," said Sancho.

"Knights-errant knew and ought to know everything, Sancho," said Don Quixote; "for there were knights-errant in former times as well qualified to deliver a sermon or discourse in the middle of an encampment, as if they had graduated in the University of Paris; whereby we may see that the lance has never blunted the pen, nor the pen the lance."

"Well, be it as your worship says," replied Sancho; "let us be off now and find some place of shelter for the night, and God grant it may be somewhere where there are no blankets, nor blanketeers, nor phantoms, nor enchanted Moors; for if there are, may the devil take the whole concern."

"Ask that of God, my son," said Don Quixote; "and do thou lead on where thou wilt, for this time I leave our lodging to thy choice; but reach me here thy hand, and feel with thy finger, and find out how many of my teeth and grinders are missing from this right side of the upper jaw, for it is there I feel the pain."

Sancho put in his fingers, and feeling about asked him, "How many grinders used your worship have on this side?"

"Four," replied Don Quixote, "besides the back-tooth, all whole and quite sound."

"Mind what you are saying, senor."

"I say four, if not five," answered Don Quixote, "for never in my life have I had tooth or grinder drawn, nor has any fallen out or been destroyed by any decay or rheum."

"Well, then," said Sancho, "in this lower side your worship has no more than two grinders and a half, and in the upper neither a half nor any at all, for it is all as smooth as the palm of my hand."

"Luckless that I am!" said Don Quixote, hearing the sad news his squire gave him; "I had rather they despoiled me of an arm, so it were not the sword-arm; for I tell thee, Sancho, a mouth without teeth is like a mill without a millstone, and a tooth is much more to be prized than a diamond; but we who profess the austere order of chivalry are liable to all this. Mount, friend, and lead the way, and I will follow thee at whatever pace thou wilt."

Sancho did as he bade him, and proceeded in the direction in which he thought he might find refuge without quitting the high road, which was there very much frequented. As they went along, then, at a slow pace—for the pain in Don Quixote's jaws kept him uneasy and ill-disposed for speed—Sancho thought it well to amuse and divert him by talk of some kind, and among the things he said to him was that which will be told in the following chapter.

CHAPTER XIX.

OF THE SHREWD DISCOURSE WHICH SANCHO HELD WITH HIS MASTER, AND OF THE ADVENTURE THAT BEFELL HIM WITH A DEAD BODY, TOGETHER WITH OTHER NOTABLE OCCURRENCES

"It seems to me, senor, that all these mishaps that have befallen us of late have been without any doubt a punishment for the offence committed by your worship against the order of chivalry in not keeping the oath you made not to eat bread off a tablecloth or embrace the queen, and all the rest of it that your worship swore to observe until you had taken that helmet of Malandrino's, or whatever the Moor is called, for I do not very well remember."

"Thou art very right, Sancho," said Don Quixote, "but to tell the truth, it had escaped my memory; and likewise thou mayest rely upon it that the affair of the blanket happened to thee because of thy fault in not reminding me of it in time; but I will make amends, for there are ways of compounding for everything in the order of chivalry."

"Why! have I taken an oath of some sort, then?" said Sancho.

"It makes no matter that thou hast not taken an oath," said Don Quixote; "suffice it that I see thou art not quite clear of complicity; and whether or no, it will not be ill done to provide ourselves with a remedy."

"In that case," said Sancho, "mind that your worship does not forget this as you did the oath; perhaps the phantoms may take it into their heads to amuse themselves once more with me; or even with your worship if they see you so obstinate."

While engaged in this and other talk, night overtook them on the road before they had reached or discovered any place of shelter; and what made it still worse was that they were dying of hunger, for with the loss of the alforjas they had lost their entire larder and commissariat; and to complete the misfortune they met with an adventure which without any invention had really the appearance of one. It so happened that the night closed in somewhat darkly, but for all that they pushed on, Sancho feeling sure that as the road was the king's highway they might reasonably expect to find some inn within a league or two. Going along, then, in this way, the night dark, the squire hungry, the master sharp-set, they saw coming towards them on the road they were travelling a great number of lights which looked exactly like stars in motion. Sancho was taken aback at the sight of them, nor did Don Quixote altogether relish them: the one pulled up his ass by the halter, the other his hack by the bridle, and they stood still, watching anxiously to see what all this would turn out to be, and found that the lights were approaching them, and the nearer they came the greater they seemed, at which spectacle Sancho began to shake like a man dosed with mercury, and Don Quixote's hair stood on end; he, however, plucking up spirit a little, said:

"This, no doubt, Sancho, will be a most mighty and perilous adventure, in which it will be needful for me to put forth all my valour and resolution."

"Unlucky me!" answered Sancho; "if this adventure happens to be one of phantoms, as I am beginning to think it is, where shall I find the ribs to bear it?"

"Be they phantoms ever so much," said Don Quixote, "I will not permit them to touch a thread of thy garments; for if they played tricks with thee the time before, it was because I was unable to leap the walls of the yard; but now we are on a wide plain, where I shall be able to wield my sword as I please."

"And if they enchant and cripple you as they did the last time," said

Sancho, "what difference will it make being on the open plain or not?"

"For all that," replied Don Quixote, "I entreat thee, Sancho, to keep a good heart, for experience will tell thee what mine is."

"I will, please God," answered Sancho, and the two retiring to one side of the road set themselves to observe closely what all these moving lights might be; and very soon afterwards they made out some twenty encamisados, all on horseback, with lighted torches in their hands, the awe-inspiring aspect of whom completely extinguished the courage of Sancho, who began to chatter with his teeth like one in the cold fit of an ague; and his heart sank and his teeth chattered still more when they perceived distinctly that behind them there came a litter covered over with black and followed by six more mounted figures in mourning down to the very feet of their mules—for they could perceive plainly they were not horses by the easy pace at which they went. And as the encamisados came along they muttered to themselves in a low plaintive tone. This strange spectacle at such an hour and in such a solitary place was quite enough to strike terror into Sancho's heart, and even into his master's; and (save in Don Quixote's case) did so, for all Sancho's resolution had now broken down. It was just the opposite with his master, whose imagination immediately conjured up all this to him vividly as one of the adventures of his books.

He took it into his head that the litter was a bier on which was borne some sorely wounded or slain knight, to avenge whom was a task reserved for him alone; and without any further reasoning he laid his lance in rest, fixed himself firmly in his saddle, and with gallant spirit and bearing took up his position in the middle of the road where the encamisados must of necessity pass; and as soon as he saw them near at hand he raised his voice and said:

"Halt, knights, or whosoever ye may be, and render me account of who ye are, whence ye come, where ye go, what it is ye carry upon that bier, for, to judge by appearances, either ye have done some wrong or some wrong has been done to you, and it is fitting and necessary that I should know, either that I may chastise you for the evil ye have done, or else that I may avenge you for the injury that has been inflicted upon you."

"We are in haste," answered one of the encamisados, "and the inn is far off, and we cannot stop to render you such an account as you demand;" and spurring his mule he moved on.

Don Quixote was mightily provoked by this answer, and seizing the mule by the bridle he said, "Halt, and be more mannerly, and render an account of what I have asked of you; else, take my defiance to combat, all of you."

The mule was shy, and was so frightened at her bridle being seized that rearing up she flung her rider to the ground over her haunches. An attendant who was on foot, seeing the encamisado fall, began to abuse Don Quixote, who now moved to anger, without any more ado, laying his lance in rest charged one of the men in mourning and brought him badly wounded to the ground, and as he wheeled round upon the others the agility with which he attacked and routed them was a sight to see, for it seemed just as if wings had that instant grown upon Rocinante, so lightly and proudly did he bear himself. The encamisados were all timid folk and unarmed, so they speedily made their escape from the fray and set off at a run across the plain with their lighted torches, looking exactly like maskers running on some gala or festival night. The mourners, too, enveloped and swathed in their skirts and gowns, were unable to bestir themselves, and so with entire safety to himself Don Quixote belaboured them all and drove them off against their will, for they all thought it was no man but a devil from hell come to carry away the dead body they had in the litter.

Sancho beheld all this in astonishment at the intrepidity of his lord, and said to himself, "Clearly this master of mine is as bold and valiant as he says he is."

A burning torch lay on the ground near the first man whom the mule had thrown, by the light of which Don Quixote perceived him, and coming up to him he presented the point of the lance to his face, calling on him to yield himself prisoner, or else he would kill him; to which the prostrate man replied, "I am prisoner enough as it is; I cannot stir, for one of my legs is broken: I entreat you, if you be a Christian gentleman, not to kill me, which will be committing grave sacrilege, for I am a licentiate and I hold first orders."

"Then what the devil brought you here, being a churchman?" said Don

Quixote.

"What, senor?" said the other. "My bad luck."

"Then still worse awaits you," said Don Quixote, "if you do not satisfy me as to all I asked you at first."

"You shall be soon satisfied," said the licentiate; "you must know, then, that though just now I said I was a licentiate, I am only a bachelor, and my name is Alonzo Lopez; I am a native of Alcobendas, I come from the city of Baeza with eleven others, priests, the same who fled with the torches, and we are going to the city of Segovia accompanying a dead body which is in that litter, and is that of a gentleman who died in Baeza, where he was interred; and now, as I said, we are taking his bones to their burial-place, which is in Segovia, where he was born."

"And who killed him?" asked Don Quixote.

"God, by means of a malignant fever that took him," answered the bachelor.

"In that case," said Don Quixote, "the Lord has relieved me of the task of avenging his death had any other slain him; but, he who slew him having slain him, there is nothing for it but to be silent, and shrug one's shoulders; I should do the same were he to slay myself; and I would have your reverence know that I am a knight of La Mancha, Don Quixote by name, and it is my business and calling to roam the world righting wrongs and redressing injuries."

"I do not know how that about righting wrongs can be," said the bachelor, "for from straight you have made me crooked, leaving me with a broken leg that will never see itself straight again all the days of its life; and the injury you have redressed in my case has been to leave me injured in such a way that I shall remain injured for ever; and the height of misadventure it was to fall in with you who go in search of adventures."

"Things do not all happen in the same way," answered Don Quixote; "it all came, Sir Bachelor Alonzo Lopez, of your going, as you did, by night, dressed in those surplices, with lighted torches, praying, covered with mourning, so that naturally you looked like something evil and of the other world; and so I could not avoid doing my duty in attacking you, and I should have attacked you even had I known positively that you were the very devils of hell, for such I certainly believed and took you to be."

"As my fate has so willed it," said the bachelor, "I entreat you, sir knight-errant, whose errand has been such an evil one for me, to help me to get from under this mule that holds one of my legs caught between the stirrup and the saddle."

"I would have talked on till to-morrow," said Don Quixote; "how long were you going to wait before telling me of your distress?"

He at once called to Sancho, who, however, had no mind to come, as he was just then engaged in unloading a sumpter mule, well laden with provender, which these worthy gentlemen had brought with them. Sancho made a bag of his coat, and, getting together as much as he could, and as the bag would hold, he loaded his beast, and then hastened to obey his master's call, and helped him to remove the bachelor from under the mule; then putting him on her back he gave him the torch, and Don Quixote bade him follow the track of his companions, and beg pardon of them on his part for the wrong which he could not help doing them.

And said Sancho, "If by chance these gentlemen should want to know who was the hero that served them so, your worship may tell them that he is the famous Don Quixote of La Mancha, otherwise called the Knight of the Rueful Countenance."

The bachelor then took his departure.

I forgot to mention that before he did so he said to Don Quixote, "Remember that you stand excommunicated for having laid violent hands on a holy thing, juxta illud, si quis, suadente diabolo."

"I do not understand that Latin," answered Don Quixote, "but I know well I did not lay hands, only this pike; besides, I did not think I was committing an assault upon priests or things of the Church, which, like a Catholic and faithful Christian as I am, I respect and revere, but upon phantoms and spectres of the other world; but even so, I remember how it fared with Cid Ruy Diaz when he broke the chair of the ambassador of that king before his Holiness the Pope, who excommunicated him for the same; and yet the good Roderick of Vivar bore himself that day like a very noble and valiant knight."

On hearing this the bachelor took his departure, as has been said, without making any reply; and Don Quixote asked Sancho what had induced him to call him the "Knight of the Rueful Countenance" more then than at any other time.

"I will tell you," answered Sancho; "it was because I have been looking at you for some time by the light of the torch held by that unfortunate, and verily your worship has got of late the most ill-favoured countenance I ever saw: it must be either owing to the fatigue of this combat, or else to the want of teeth and grinders."

"It is not that," replied Don Quixote, "but because the sage whose duty it will be to write the history of my achievements must have thought it proper that I should take some distinctive name as all knights of yore did; one being 'He of the Burning Sword,' another 'He of the Unicorn,' this one 'He of the Damsels,' that 'He of the Phoenix,' another 'The Knight of the Griffin,' and another 'He of the Death,' and by these names and designations they were known all the world round; and so I say that the sage aforesaid must have put it into your mouth and mind just now to call me 'The Knight of the Rueful Countenance,' as I intend to call myself from this day forward; and that the said name may fit me better, I mean, when the opportunity offers, to have a very rueful countenance painted on my shield."

"There is no occasion, senor, for wasting time or money on making that countenance," said Sancho; "for all that need be done is for your worship to show your own, face to face, to those who look at you, and without anything more, either image or shield, they will call you 'Him of the Rueful Countenance' and believe me I am telling you the truth, for I assure you, senor (and in good part be it said), hunger and the loss of your grinders have given you such an ill-favoured face that, as I say, the rueful picture may be very well spared."

Don Quixote laughed at Sancho's pleasantry; nevertheless he resolved to call himself by that name, and have his shield or buckler painted as he had devised.

Don Quixote would have looked to see whether the body in the litter were bones or not, but Sancho would not have it, saying:

"Senor, you have ended this perilous adventure more safely for yourself than any of those I have seen: perhaps these people, though beaten and routed, may bethink themselves that it is a single man that has beaten them, and feeling sore and ashamed of it may take heart and come in search of us and give us trouble enough. The ass is in proper trim, the mountains are near at hand, hunger presses, we have nothing more to do but make good our retreat, and, as the saying is, the dead to the grave and the living to the loaf."

And driving his ass before him he begged his master to follow, who, feeling that Sancho was right, did so without replying; and after proceeding some little distance between two hills they found themselves in a wide and retired valley, where they alighted, and Sancho unloaded his beast, and stretched upon the green grass, with hunger for sauce, they breakfasted, dined, lunched, and supped all at once, satisfying their appetites with more than one store of cold meat which the dead man's clerical gentlemen (who seldom put themselves on short allowance) had brought with them on their sumpter mule. But another piece of ill-luck befell them, which Sancho held the worst of all, and that was that they had no wine to drink, nor even water to moisten their lips; and as thirst tormented them, Sancho, observing that the meadow where they were was full of green and tender grass, said what will be told in the following chapter.

CHAPTER XX.

OF THE UNEXAMPLED AND UNHEARD-OF ADVENTURE WHICH WAS ACHIEVED BY THE VALIANT DON QUIXOTE OF LA MANCHA WITH LESS PERIL THAN ANY EVER ACHIEVED BY ANY FAMOUS KNIGHT IN THE WORLD

"It cannot be, senor, but that this grass is a proof that there must be hard by some spring or brook to give it moisture, so it would be well to move a little farther on, that we may find some place where we may quench this terrible thirst that plagues us, which beyond a doubt is more distressing than hunger."

The advice seemed good to Don Quixote, and, he leading Rocinante by the bridle and Sancho the ass by the halter, after he had packed away upon him the remains of the supper, they advanced the meadow feeling their way, for the darkness of the night made it impossible to see anything; but they had not gone two hundred paces when a loud noise of water, as if falling from great rocks, struck their ears. The sound cheered them greatly; but halting to make out by listening from what quarter it came they heard unseasonably another noise which spoiled the satisfaction the sound of the water gave them, especially for Sancho, who was by nature timid and faint-hearted. They heard, I say, strokes falling with a measured beat, and a certain rattling of iron and chains that, together with the furious din of the water, would have struck terror into any heart but Don Quixote's. The night was, as has been said, dark, and they had happened to reach a spot in among some tall trees, whose leaves stirred by a gentle breeze made a low ominous sound; so that, what with the solitude, the place, the darkness, the noise of the water, and the rustling of the leaves, everything inspired awe and dread; more especially as they perceived that the strokes did not cease, nor the wind lull, nor morning approach; to all which might be added their ignorance as to where they were.

But Don Quixote, supported by his intrepid heart, leaped on Rocinante, and bracing his buckler on his arm, brought his pike to the slope, and said, "Friend Sancho, know that I by Heaven's will have been born in this our iron age to revive in it the age of gold, or the golden as it is called; I am he for whom perils, mighty achievements, and valiant deeds are reserved; I am, I say again, he who is to revive the Knights of the Round Table, the Twelve of France and the Nine Worthies; and he who is to consign to oblivion the Platirs, the Tablantes, the Olivantes and Tirantes, the Phoebuses and Belianises, with the whole herd of famous knights-errant of days gone by, performing in these in which I live such exploits, marvels, and feats of arms as shall obscure their brightest deeds. Thou dost mark well, faithful and trusty squire, the gloom of this night, its strange silence, the dull confused murmur of those trees, the awful sound of that water in quest of which we came, that seems as though it were precipitating and dashing itself down from the lofty mountains of the Moon, and that incessant hammering that wounds and pains our ears; which things all together and each of itself are enough to instil fear, dread, and dismay into the breast of Mars himself, much more into one not used to hazards and adventures of the kind. Well, then, all this that I put before thee is but an incentive and stimulant to my spirit, making my heart burst in my bosom through eagerness to engage in this adventure, arduous as it promises to be; therefore tighten Rocinante's girths a little, and God be with thee; wait for me here three days and no more, and if in that time I come not back, thou canst return to our village, and thence, to do me a favour and a service, thou wilt go to El Toboso, where thou shalt say to my incomparable lady Dulcinea that her captive knight hath died in attempting things that might make him worthy of being called hers."

When Sancho heard his master's words he began to weep in the most pathetic way, saying:

"Senor, I know not why your worship wants to attempt this so dreadful adventure; it is night now, no one sees us here, we can easily turn about and take ourselves out of danger, even if we don't drink for three days to come; and as there is no one to see us, all the less will there be anyone to set us down as cowards; besides, I have many a time heard the curate of our village, whom your worship knows well, preach that he who seeks danger perishes in it; so it is not right to tempt God by trying so tremendous a feat from which there can be no escape save by a miracle, and Heaven has performed enough of them for your worship in delivering you from being blanketed as I was, and bringing you out victorious and safe and sound from among all those enemies that were with the dead man; and if all this does not move or soften that hard heart, let this thought and reflection move it, that you will have hardly quitted this spot when from pure fear I shall yield my soul up to anyone that will take it. I left home and wife and children to come and serve your worship, trusting to do better and not worse; but as covetousness bursts the bag, it has rent my hopes asunder, for just as I had them highest about getting that wretched unlucky island your worship has so often promised me, I see that instead and in lieu of it you mean to desert me now in a place so far from human reach: for God's sake, master mine, deal not so unjustly by me, and if your worship will not entirely give up attempting this feat, at least put it off till morning, for by what the lore I learned when I was a shepherd tells me it cannot want three hours of dawn now, because the mouth of the Horn is overhead and makes midnight in the line of the left arm."

"How canst thou see, Sancho," said Don Quixote, "where it makes that line, or where this mouth or this occiput is that thou talkest of, when the night is so dark that there is not a star to be seen in the whole heaven?"

"That's true," said Sancho, "but fear has sharp eyes, and sees things underground, much more above in heavens; besides, there is good reason to show that it now wants but little of day."

"Let it want what it may," replied Don Quixote, "it shall not be said of me now or at any time that tears or entreaties turned me aside from doing what was in accordance with knightly usage; and so I beg of thee, Sancho, to hold thy peace, for God, who has put it into my heart to undertake now this so unexampled and terrible adventure, will take care to watch over my safety and console thy sorrow; what thou hast to do is to tighten Rocinante's girths well, and wait here, for I shall come back shortly, alive or dead."

Sancho perceiving it his master's final resolve, and how little his tears, counsels, and entreaties prevailed with him, determined to have recourse to his own ingenuity and compel him, if he could, to wait till daylight; and so, while tightening the girths of the horse, he quietly and without being felt, with his ass' halter tied both Rocinante's legs, so that when Don Quixote strove to go he was unable as the horse could only move by jumps. Seeing the success of his trick, Sancho Panza said:

"See there, senor! Heaven, moved by my tears and prayers, has so ordered it that Rocinante cannot stir; and if you will be obstinate, and spur and strike him, you will only provoke fortune, and kick, as they say, against the pricks."

Don Quixote at this grew desperate, but the more he drove his heels into the horse, the less he stirred him; and not having any suspicion of the tying, he was fain to resign himself and wait till daybreak or until Rocinante could move, firmly persuaded that all this came of something other than Sancho's ingenuity. So he said to him, "As it is so, Sancho, and as Rocinante cannot move, I am content to wait till dawn smiles upon us, even though I weep while it delays its coming."

"There is no need to weep," answered Sancho, "for I will amuse your worship by telling stories from this till daylight, unless indeed you like to dismount and lie down to sleep a little on the green grass after the fashion of knights-errant, so as to be fresher when day comes and the moment arrives for attempting this extraordinary adventure you are looking forward to."

"What art thou talking about dismounting or sleeping for?" said Don Quixote. "Am I, thinkest thou, one of those knights that take their rest in the presence of danger? Sleep thou who art born to sleep, or do as thou wilt, for I will act as I think most consistent with my character."

"Be not angry, master mine," replied Sancho, "I did not mean to say that;" and coming close to him he laid one hand on the pommel of the saddle and the other on the cantle so that he held his master's left thigh in his embrace, not daring to separate a finger's width from him; so much afraid was he of the strokes which still resounded with a regular beat. Don Quixote bade him tell some story to amuse him as he had proposed, to which Sancho replied that he would if his dread of what he heard would let him; "Still," said he, "I will strive to tell a story which, if I can manage to relate it, and nobody interferes with the telling, is the best of stories, and let your worship give me your attention, for here I begin. What was, was; and may the good that is to come be for all, and the evil for him who goes to look for it—your worship must know that the beginning the old folk used to put to their tales was not just as each one pleased; it was a maxim of Cato Zonzorino the Roman, that says 'the evil for him that goes to look for it,' and it comes as pat to the purpose now as ring to finger, to show that your worship should keep quiet and not go looking for evil in any quarter, and that we should go back by some other road, since nobody forces us to follow this in which so many terrors affright us."

"Go on with thy story, Sancho," said Don Quixote, "and leave the choice of our road to my care."

"I say then," continued Sancho, "that in a village of Estremadura there was a goat-shepherd—that is to say, one who tended goats—which shepherd or goatherd, as my story goes, was called Lope Ruiz, and this Lope Ruiz was in love with a shepherdess called Torralva, which shepherdess called Torralva was the daughter of a rich grazier, and this rich grazier-"

"If that is the way thou tellest thy tale, Sancho," said Don Quixote, "repeating twice all thou hast to say, thou wilt not have done these two days; go straight on with it, and tell it like a reasonable man, or else say nothing."

"Tales are always told in my country in the very way I am telling this," answered Sancho, "and I cannot tell it in any other, nor is it right of your worship to ask me to make new customs."

"Tell it as thou wilt," replied Don Quixote; "and as fate will have it that I cannot help listening to thee, go on."

"And so, lord of my soul," continued Sancho, as I have said, this shepherd was in love with Torralva the shepherdess, who was a wild buxom lass with something of the look of a man about her, for she had little moustaches; I fancy I see her now."

"Then you knew her?" said Don Quixote.

"I did not know her," said Sancho, "but he who told me the story said it was so true and certain that when I told it to another I might safely declare and swear I had seen it all myself. And so in course of time, the devil, who never sleeps and puts everything in confusion, contrived that the love the shepherd bore the shepherdess turned into hatred and ill-will, and the reason, according to evil tongues, was some little jealousy she caused him that crossed the line and trespassed on forbidden ground; and so much did the shepherd hate her from that time forward that, in order to escape from her, he determined to quit the country and go where he should never set eyes on her again. Torralva, when she found herself spurned by Lope, was immediately smitten with love for him, though she had never loved him before."

"That is the natural way of women," said Don Quixote, "to scorn the one that loves them, and love the one that hates them: go on, Sancho."

"It came to pass," said Sancho, "that the shepherd carried out his intention, and driving his goats before him took his way across the plains of Estremadura to pass over into the Kingdom of Portugal. Torralva, who knew of it, went after him, and on foot and barefoot followed him at a distance, with a pilgrim's staff in her hand and a scrip round her neck, in which she carried, it is said, a bit of looking-glass and a piece of a comb and some little pot or other of paint for her face; but let her carry what she did, I am not going to trouble myself to prove it; all I say is, that the shepherd, they say, came with his flock to cross over the river Guadiana, which was at that time swollen and almost overflowing its banks, and at the spot he came to there was neither ferry nor boat nor anyone to carry him or his flock to the other side, at which he was much vexed, for he perceived that Torralva was approaching and would give him great annoyance with her tears and entreaties; however, he went looking about so closely that he discovered a fisherman who had alongside of him a boat so small that it could only hold one person and one goat; but for all that he spoke to him and agreed with him to carry himself and his three hundred goats across. The fisherman got into the boat and carried one goat over; he came back and carried another over; he came back again, and again brought over another—let your worship keep count of the goats the fisherman is taking across, for if one escapes the memory there will be an end of the story, and it will be impossible to tell another word of it. To proceed, I must tell you the landing place on the other side was miry and slippery, and the fisherman lost a great deal of time in going and coming; still he returned for another goat, and another, and another."

"Take it for granted he brought them all across," said Don Quixote, "and don't keep going and coming in this way, or thou wilt not make an end of bringing them over this twelvemonth."

"How many have gone across so far?" said Sancho.

"How the devil do I know?" replied Don Quixote.

"There it is," said Sancho, "what I told you, that you must keep a good count; well then, by God, there is an end of the story, for there is no going any farther."

"How can that be?" said Don Quixote; "is it so essential to the story to know to a nicety the goats that have crossed over, that if there be a mistake of one in the reckoning, thou canst not go on with it?"

"No, senor, not a bit," replied Sancho; "for when I asked your worship to tell me how many goats had crossed, and you answered you did not know, at that very instant all I had to say passed away out of my memory, and, faith, there was much virtue in it, and entertainment."

"So, then," said Don Quixote, "the story has come to an end?"

"As much as my mother has," said Sancho.

"In truth," said Don Quixote, "thou hast told one of the rarest stories, tales, or histories, that anyone in the world could have imagined, and such a way of telling it and ending it was never seen nor will be in a lifetime; though I expected nothing else from thy excellent understanding. But I do not wonder, for perhaps those ceaseless strokes may have confused thy wits."

"All that may be," replied Sancho, "but I know that as to my story, all that can be said is that it ends there where the mistake in the count of the passage of the goats begins."

"Let it end where it will, well and good," said Don Quixote, "and let us see if Rocinante can go;" and again he spurred him, and again Rocinante made jumps and remained where he was, so well tied was he.

Just then, whether it was the cold of the morning that was now approaching, or that he had eaten something laxative at supper, or that it was only natural (as is most likely), Sancho felt a desire to do what no one could do for him; but so great was the fear that had penetrated his heart, he dared not separate himself from his master by as much as the black of his nail; to escape doing what he wanted was, however, also impossible; so what he did for peace's sake was to remove his right hand, which held the back of the saddle, and with it to untie gently and silently the running string which alone held up his breeches, so that on loosening it they at once fell down round his feet like fetters; he then raised his shirt as well as he could and bared his hind quarters, no slim ones. But, this accomplished, which he fancied was all he had to do to get out of this terrible strait and embarrassment, another still greater difficulty presented itself, for it seemed to him impossible to relieve himself without making some noise, and he ground his teeth and squeezed his shoulders together, holding his breath as much as he could; but in spite of his precautions he was unlucky enough after all to make a little noise, very different from that which was causing him so much fear.

Don Quixote, hearing it, said, "What noise is that, Sancho?"

"I don't know, senor," said he; "it must be something new, for adventures and misadventures never begin with a trifle." Once more he tried his luck, and succeeded so well, that without any further noise or disturbance he found himself relieved of the burden that had given him so much discomfort. But as Don Quixote's sense of smell was as acute as his hearing, and as Sancho was so closely linked with him that the fumes rose almost in a straight line, it could not be but that some should reach his nose, and as soon as they did he came to its relief by compressing it between his fingers, saying in a rather snuffing tone, "Sancho, it strikes me thou art in great fear."

"I am," answered Sancho; "but how does your worship perceive it now more than ever?"

"Because just now thou smellest stronger than ever, and not of ambergris," answered Don Quixote.

"Very likely," said Sancho, "but that's not my fault, but your worship's, for leading me about at unseasonable hours and at such unwonted paces."

"Then go back three or four, my friend," said Don Quixote, all the time with his fingers to his nose; "and for the future pay more attention to thy person and to what thou owest to mine; for it is my great familiarity with thee that has bred this contempt."

"I'll bet," replied Sancho, "that your worship thinks I have done something I ought not with my person."

"It makes it worse to stir it, friend Sancho," returned Don Quixote.

With this and other talk of the same sort master and man passed the night, till Sancho, perceiving that daybreak was coming on apace, very cautiously untied Rocinante and tied up his breeches. As soon as Rocinante found himself free, though by nature he was not at all mettlesome, he seemed to feel lively and began pawing—for as to capering, begging his pardon, he knew not what it meant. Don Quixote, then, observing that Rocinante could move, took it as a good sign and a signal that he should attempt the dread adventure. By this time day had fully broken and everything showed distinctly, and Don Quixote saw that he was among some tall trees, chestnuts, which cast a very deep shade; he perceived likewise that the sound of the strokes did not cease, but could not discover what caused it, and so without any further delay he let Rocinante feel the spur, and once more taking leave of Sancho, he told him to wait for him there three days at most, as he had said before, and if he should not have returned by that time, he might feel sure it had been God's will that he should end his days in that perilous adventure. He again repeated the message and commission with which he was to go on his behalf to his lady Dulcinea, and said he was not to be uneasy as to the payment of his services, for before leaving home he had made his will, in which he would find himself fully recompensed in the matter of wages in due proportion to the time he had served; but if God delivered him safe, sound, and unhurt out of that danger, he might look upon the promised island as much more than certain. Sancho began to weep afresh on again hearing the affecting words of his good master, and resolved to stay with him until the final issue and end of the business. From these tears and this honourable resolve of Sancho Panza's the author of this history infers that he must have been of good birth and at least an old Christian; and the feeling he displayed touched his but not so much as to make him show any weakness; on the contrary, hiding what he felt as well as he could, he began to move towards that quarter whence the sound of the water and of the strokes seemed to come.

Sancho followed him on foot, leading by the halter, as his custom was, his ass, his constant comrade in prosperity or adversity; and advancing some distance through the shady chestnut trees they came upon a little meadow at the foot of some high rocks, down which a mighty rush of water flung itself. At the foot of the rocks were some rudely constructed houses looking more like ruins than houses, from among which came, they perceived, the din and clatter of blows, which still continued without intermission. Rocinante took fright at the noise of the water and of the blows, but quieting him Don Quixote advanced step by step towards the houses, commending himself with all his heart to his lady, imploring her support in that dread pass and enterprise, and on the way commending himself to God, too, not to forget him. Sancho who never quitted his side, stretched his neck as far as he could and peered between the legs of Rocinante to see if he could now discover what it was that caused him such fear and apprehension. They went it might be a hundred paces farther, when on turning a corner the true cause, beyond the possibility of any mistake, of that dread-sounding and to them awe-inspiring noise that had kept them all the night in such fear and perplexity, appeared plain and obvious; and it was (if, reader, thou art not disgusted and disappointed) six fulling hammers which by their alternate strokes made all the din.

When Don Quixote perceived what it was, he was struck dumb and rigid from head to foot. Sancho glanced at him and saw him with his head bent down upon his breast in manifest mortification; and Don Quixote glanced at Sancho and saw him with his cheeks puffed out and his mouth full of laughter, and evidently ready to explode with it, and in spite of his vexation he could not help laughing at the sight of him; and when Sancho saw his master begin he let go so heartily that he had to hold his sides with both hands to keep himself from bursting with laughter. Four times he stopped, and as many times did his laughter break out afresh with the same violence as at first, whereat Don Quixote grew furious, above all when he heard him say mockingly, "Thou must know, friend Sancho, that of Heaven's will I was born in this our iron age to revive in it the golden or age of gold; I am he for whom are reserved perils, mighty achievements, valiant deeds;" and here he went on repeating the words that Don Quixote uttered the first time they heard the awful strokes.

Don Quixote, then, seeing that Sancho was turning him into ridicule, was so mortified and vexed that he lifted up his pike and smote him two such blows that if, instead of catching them on his shoulders, he had caught them on his head there would have been no wages to pay, unless indeed to his heirs. Sancho seeing that he was getting an awkward return in earnest for his jest, and fearing his master might carry it still further, said to him very humbly, "Calm yourself, sir, for by God I am only joking."

"Well, then, if you are joking I am not," replied Don Quixote. "Look here, my lively gentleman, if these, instead of being fulling hammers, had been some perilous adventure, have I not, think you, shown the courage required for the attempt and achievement? Am I, perchance, being, as I am, a gentleman, bound to know and distinguish sounds and tell whether they come from fulling mills or not; and that, when perhaps, as is the case, I have never in my life seen any as you have, low boor as you are, that have been born and bred among them? But turn me these six hammers into six giants, and bring them to beard me, one by one or all together, and if I do not knock them head over heels, then make what mockery you like of me."

"No more of that, senor," returned Sancho; "I own I went a little too far with the joke. But tell me, your worship, now that peace is made between us (and may God bring you out of all the adventures that may befall you as safe and sound as he has brought you out of this one), was it not a thing to laugh at, and is it not a good story, the great fear we were in?—at least that I was in; for as to your worship I see now that you neither know nor understand what either fear or dismay is."

"I do not deny," said Don Quixote, "that what happened to us may be worth laughing at, but it is not worth making a story about, for it is not everyone that is shrewd enough to hit the right point of a thing."

"At any rate," said Sancho, "your worship knew how to hit the right point with your pike, aiming at my head and hitting me on the shoulders, thanks be to God and my own smartness in dodging it. But let that pass; all will come out in the scouring; for I have heard say 'he loves thee well that makes thee weep;' and moreover that it is the way with great lords after any hard words they give a servant to give him a pair of breeches; though I do not know what they give after blows, unless it be that knights-errant after blows give islands, or kingdoms on the mainland."

"It may be on the dice," said Don Quixote, "that all thou sayest will come true; overlook the past, for thou art shrewd enough to know that our first movements are not in our own control; and one thing for the future bear in mind, that thou curb and restrain thy loquacity in my company; for in all the books of chivalry that I have read, and they are innumerable, I never met with a squire who talked so much to his lord as thou dost to thine; and in fact I feel it to be a great fault of thine and of mine: of thine, that thou hast so little respect for me; of mine, that I do not make myself more respected. There was Gandalin, the squire of Amadis of Gaul, that was Count of the Insula Firme, and we read of him that he always addressed his lord with his cap in his hand, his head bowed down and his body bent double, more turquesco. And then, what shall we say of Gasabal, the squire of Galaor, who was so silent that in order to indicate to us the greatness of his marvellous taciturnity his name is only once mentioned in the whole of that history, as long as it is truthful? From all I have said thou wilt gather, Sancho, that there must be a difference between master and man, between lord and lackey, between knight and squire: so that from this day forward in our intercourse we must observe more respect and take less liberties, for in whatever way I may be provoked with you it will be bad for the pitcher. The favours and benefits that I have promised you will come in due time, and if they do not your wages at least will not be lost, as I have already told you."

"All that your worship says is very well," said Sancho, "but I should like to know (in case the time of favours should not come, and it might be necessary to fall back upon wages) how much did the squire of a knight-errant get in those days, and did they agree by the month, or by the day like bricklayers?"

"I do not believe," replied Don Quixote, "that such squires were ever on wages, but were dependent on favour; and if I have now mentioned thine in the sealed will I have left at home, it was with a view to what may happen; for as yet I know not how chivalry will turn out in these wretched times of ours, and I do not wish my soul to suffer for trifles in the other world; for I would have thee know, Sancho, that in this there is no condition more hazardous than that of adventurers."

"That is true," said Sancho, "since the mere noise of the hammers of a fulling mill can disturb and disquiet the heart of such a valiant errant adventurer as your worship; but you may be sure I will not open my lips henceforward to make light of anything of your worship's, but only to honour you as my master and natural lord."

"By so doing," replied Don Quixote, "shalt thou live long on the face of the earth; for next to parents, masters are to be respected as though they were parents."

Made in the USA
Middletown, DE
21 October 2018